HOLLY JUNE SMITH

SEE YOU NEXT WINTER

Copyright © 2024 by Holly June Smith

All rights reserved.

The characters and events portrayed in this book are fictitious. Any similarity to real persons, living or dead, is coincidental and not intended by the author.

No part of this book may be reproduced, or stored in a retrieval system, or transmitted in any form or by any means, electronic, mechanical, photocopying, recording, or otherwise, without express written permission of the publisher.

Cover design by Gemma Flowers at The Lucky Type

Contents

Dedication	VII
A Note From Holly	IX
About the Author	XI
1. Ryan	1
2. Kayla	5
3. Ryan	12
4. Ryan	18
5. Kayla	23
6. Kayla	24
7. Ryan	32
8. Ryan	33
9. Kayla	36
10. Ryan	41
11. Ryan	44
12. Kayla	49
13. Ryan	51
14. Kayla	58
15. Kayla	61

16.	Kayla	62
17.	Ryan	68
18.	Ryan	70
19.	Ryan	75
20.	Kayla	77
21.	Ryan	84
22.	Kayla	86
23.	Kayla	90
24.	Ryan	95
25.	Kayla	97
26.	Kayla	99
27.	Ryan	102
28.	Ryan	107
29.	Ryan	111
30.	Kayla	116
31.	Kayla	122
32.	Kayla	124
33.	Kayla	127
34.	Kayla	131
35.	Ryan	136
36.	Kayla	141
37.	Kayla	144
38.	Kayla	145
39.	Ryan	147

40.	Ryan	151
41.	Ryan	156
42.	Ryan	164
43.	Kayla	167
44.	Kayla	171
45.	Kayla	175
46.	Ryan	178
47.	Kayla	182
48.	Ryan	184
49.	Kayla	186
50.	Ryan	191
51.	Ryan	195
52.	Ryan	198
53.	Kayla	199
54.	Kayla	203
55.	Kayla	207
56.	Ryan	209
57.	Ryan & Kayla	213
Acknowledgements		216
Also by Holly June Smith		219
The Best Book Boyfriend		221

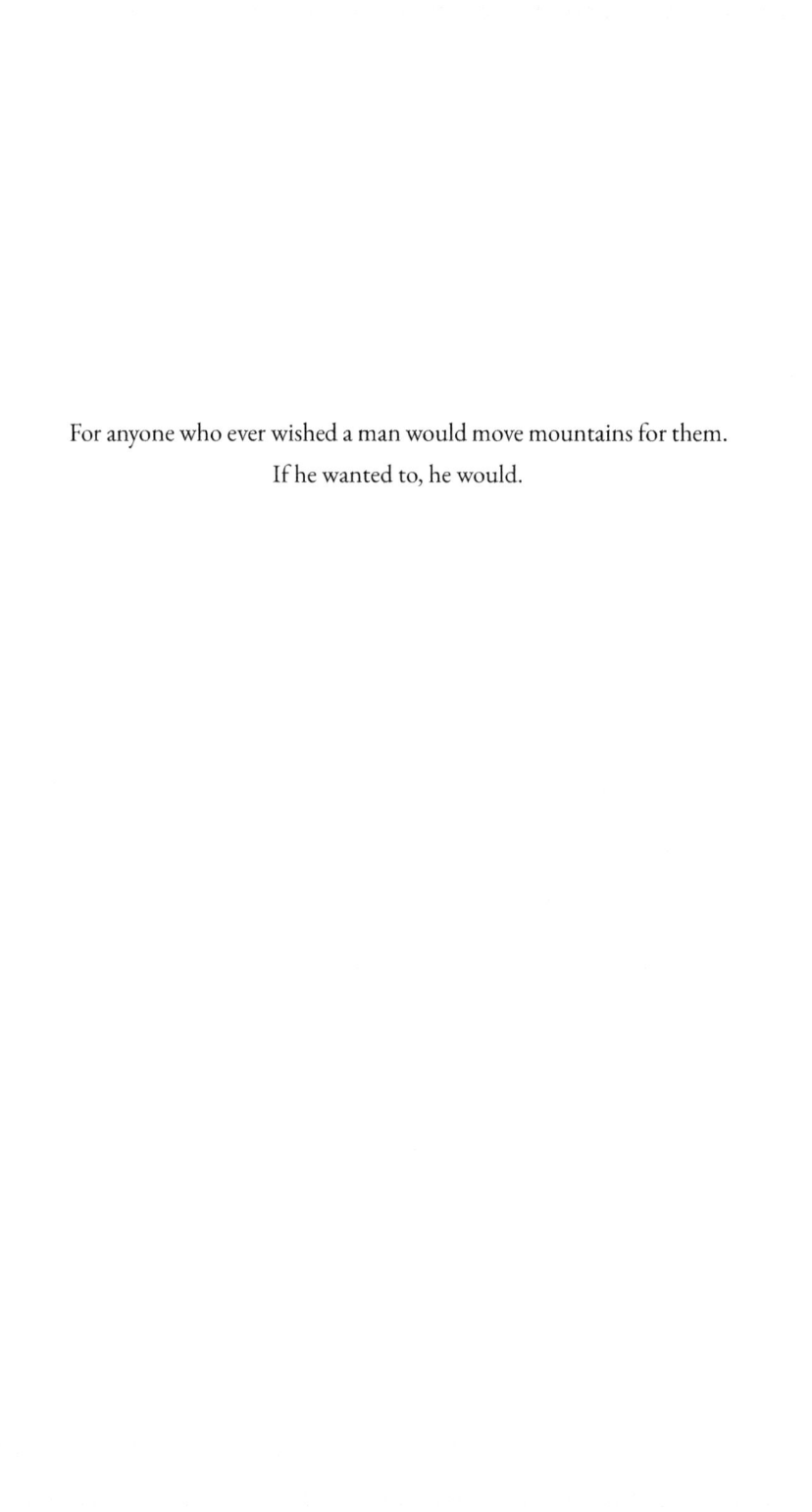

For anyone who ever wished a man would move mountains for them.
If he wanted to, he would.

A Note From Holly

Thank you for reading *See You Next Winter*. I hope you enjoy it as much as I enjoyed writing it.

Please be advised that this book is an open-door romance featuring on-page sexual content for mature readers only.

This is a fun, cosy (and spicy!) Christmas novella with low angst. It is the follow up to *Can I Tell You Something?* and can be read as a standalone, but I think you'll enjoy it more if you read that one first.

For content warnings, *See You Next Winter* contains discussion of other partners (not cheating), masked intruder play (consensual and requested), and strong language.

It also contains airport goodbyes, and those wreck me.

About the Author

Holly June Smith is a writer and romance addict who is constantly falling in love with fictional heroes and dreaming up new ones.

Holly is also a wedding celebrant who helps couples celebrate their beautiful real-life love stories.

Originally from the North East of Scotland, she now lives in Hertfordshire, England, with her partner, their two children, and a TBR that threatens to crush her in her sleep.

You can find her online @hollyjunesmith or join the Holly June Smith Reader Group on Facebook.

Chapter 1
Ryan

The best things about Christmas are snow, skiing, and sneaking around with Kayla McInnes.

My family has spent every winter break since I was born at our chalet in the French Alps, and since her family owns a chalet nearby, it was inevitable we'd become friends.

As kids, our sneaking meant nabbing extra sugar cookies and chocolate coins, or heading off-piste to find adventure in hidden trails and woods. For the past decade, it's meant stolen kisses and hurried orgasms whenever we've had the chance to slip away from our family festivities.

Except, I've skipped out on the last two years, and since we don't keep in touch when we're not in the mountains, I have no idea how she's going to feel about seeing me again.

My mother ruffles my hair like I'm five years old and takes the chair next to me.

"I can't believe you didn't tell us you were coming."

"We didn't know ourselves until right before the flight." My body clock is still on Los Angeles time and I'm so exhausted, I'm not entirely sure this isn't a dream.

At the head of the table sits my buddy, Cameron, a born and bred Californian. He looks just as shocked as I am. We'd planned to spend the holidays surfing, not skiing. He'd never even seen snow until today.

I moved to the US for film school nearly a decade ago, but I didn't meet Cameron until I needed a second sound guy for a short I was working on a few years back. After that we ended up at the same studio, and when our leases came up around the same time, we found a two-bedroom in a great location and have lived together ever since.

He's a good friend. We live together and work together, and if it weren't for his *'you've only got one life'* attitude, we wouldn't be here at all. After a few beers on Friday, my pining for the mountains got the better of me, and next thing I knew, we were shoving clothes into bags and headed for the airport.

Over Dad's carbonara, we fill them in on what we've both been up to at the film studio. Thankfully, Cameron doesn't mention his side hustle where he jerks off into a microphone and puts it on the internet for thousands of women to hear. It's weird as fuck, but I shouldn't complain, since it paid for us to get last-minute flights to Geneva in business class.

It's nice seeing him here with my family, even though he's a total fish out of water. Mum quizzes him about his skiing experience and offers for my sister, Hannah, to give him some lessons. She trained as an instructor years ago and was supposed to do a season here until her shitty ex-boyfriend cheated on her and she cancelled all her plans.

Sitting across from me, Hannah seems quieter than usual. There are only two years between us, and though we live an ocean apart, we're still reasonably close. She checks in regularly, but these past few months I've been busy mixing a new streaming series, and I'm definitely failing in my brotherly duties.

Hannah works for our dad's entertainment law firm, but she's a perfectionist who puts way too much pressure on herself. She's struggled with her mental health in the past and though she looks fine, something feels off. She's barely made eye-contact with me or Cameron since we arrived.

After dinner, Mum and Dad take their wine to the sofa while us kids clear the table. Hannah rinses plates and I stack them in the dishwasher.

"Does Kayla know you're here?" she asks.

"No, I'm hoping I can surprise her."

"Who's Kayla?" Cameron asks behind us, and Hannah's head snaps in my direction.

"You haven't told him about Kayla?"

"She's my mountain friend," I shrug. "What is there to say?"

I've never known how to label Kayla. She's not a girlfriend, even though she's everything I'd want from one. She's a friend, but I go months—*years*—without talking to her, then we do decidedly un-friendly things whenever we're together. Fuck buddies doesn't come close to what we are. She's the first place my mind goes in the quiet moments.

She's my soulmate.

I shove a leftover piece of garlic bread in my mouth and don't let myself think about it.

"Dude, what the fuck is a mountain friend?"

"She's our friend who spends Christmas here too," Hannah tells him. "We always meet up when we're all in town."

Cam bursts out laughing, smacking me in the chest with the back of his hand. "Oh, thank god. Bro, I thought you were about to tell me you were friends with a troll or something."

"You've read too many fairytales," I laugh.

"Can you blame me? This place is like Narnia. I saw those forests on the drive over. There's no way they don't have creatures living in them."

Hannah stares at him like she's trying to figure out if my friend has rocks in his head. Eventually, she snaps out of her trance and focuses her attention back on me. "Are you going to see her tonight?"

"Nah, think I'll show Cam the hot tub and find her after I've caught up on sleep. You joining us?"

"Nope," she says quickly, heading for the door and disappearing upstairs. Something is definitely up with her. I'm going to figure it out, but first, beers under the stars with my bro.

Chapter 2
Kayla

Rico's bar is as busy as you'd expect it to be this close to Christmas. Half the patrons are still sporting sweaty t-shirts and ski pants, and clearly came straight here after the last run of the day. A chorus of heavy boots stomps across the floor whenever they need a fresh round of drinks.

The other half at least made the effort to go home and shower, throw on something clean, and come back without helmet hair. Some nights I'm in the first camp, but tonight it's the latter.

In the past, this would be the day I'd finish school in Edinburgh and fly out to Geneva with my parents. From there, Dad would hire a car, and we'd make the two-hour journey through mountain towns, up steep winding roads, to the little Alpine village where my family has owned a ski chalet since long before I was born.

When I was a child, all I cared about was getting out of the car and catching my first snowflake on my tongue. That and drinking as many thick, rich hot chocolates as possible before we had to fly home again.

As a teenager, I was more interested in hitting the slopes, getting up early to catch the first chairlift with my dad, cruising those wide open, freshly groomed pistes, feeling like we were the only two people in the world. I loved ice skating in the town square, the festive lights, the parade and all the local traditions.

Then I grew up, and the only thing I cared about was Ryan Richmond. Over two decades of winters, my childhood chairlift buddy became the man my body craved for weeks in the run up to Christmas. As soon as we packed away our Halloween decorations, he became all I could think about. My friends back home thought I was nuts pining over a boy I only ever saw on holiday, but being with him always felt like coming home.

Unfortunately, my Christmas holiday fling didn't fly out last year, nor the year before that, and when I bumped into his parents in the supermarket a few days ago, they smiled wanly and told me he won't be here this year either.

Which is fine. It's not like he owes me anything, and it's certainly not like I'll have trouble finding someone else to have a little fun with. Let's hope it's someone who showered.

The queue for the bar is three deep, but I know from experience it's easier to get to the front if you push into the dead spot in the middle. By the time I'm pressed against the sticky bar, one of the staff will recognise me and serve me next. Rico's is the spot I tell all my clients to head to at the end of a long day on the slopes, so getting a cold beer in my hand quickly is the least they can do.

And I need that beer so I can run my game.

The one where I tug one of my long blonde pigtails loose, weave through the crowd until someone catches my eye, then ask them to hold my beer while I fix it. It's cute watching them panic when I maintain eye contact with my hair-tie between my teeth. They never know whether to look at my face or my hair or my tits, but by the time I've woven those strands back into place, I have a pretty good idea whether or not they're coming home with me. It never fails.

There are plenty of people in Rico's tonight and I scan the crowd for new faces, the cute and unfamiliar. I don't think I'll have any trouble finding a substitute for the man I really want.

It can't be more than thirty seconds before I feel the weight of a body pressing in behind me. It's not an uncommon occurrence when it's this busy, but there's always a moment where you have to make a split second assessment. Is this person also trying to fight their way to the front, or am I about to be felt up by some handsy stranger who'll blame his behaviour on booze and the altitude.

I might be here to hook-up, but that's on my terms, and those terms do not include unwelcome groping.

The answer comes in the shape of a large hand resting on my hip, followed by another on the other side. My hand balls into a fist and I'm about to spin around and take a swing that may or may not get me permanently barred from Rico's, when his whisper lands against my ear.

"Hey, Bunny."

The way my body betrays me, flooding with heat and melting back against his chest, is frankly embarrassing. My eyes flutter closed and I squeeze them tighter.

Maybe if I don't look, this won't be happening. If I ignore him, he'll become a figment of my imagination. If I don't turn around, I won't get my heart broken again.

He lifts one of my long braids back over my shoulder, opening up space at my neck for him to lean in and whisper close to my ear.

"I've been looking for you everywhere."

I gulp hard, and a cold beer becomes even more of a necessity. "When did you get here?"

"Night before last."

Two whole days.

Two whole days when we could have been together. If I'd known he was here, I wouldn't be out in Rico's hoping to pick up some semi-decent guy to scratch an itch. We could have been...

My brain stops the thought before my heart takes it too far. Two days is nothing when you add them to the one-thousand plus since I last saw his face. I stopped counting a long time ago.

Twisting in his hold, I find him gazing down at me, his hair sticking up like always. His eyes are more grey than green in this light, but still so familiar. How many hours have I spent staring into them? I couldn't even tell you which ones were real and which I imagined.

The scruff of beard is new, and makes him look a little older, but no less handsome. Or maybe it's not new. How would I know since he disappeared out of my life without a word?

"You can't have been looking hard. Where did you try?"

"At your house."

"You came to my house?"

"It was totally dark. Where've you been hiding?"

His hands are still on my hips, and I feel his fingertips flex in time with his words. Fuck, I've missed sparring with him. "I was out."

"With who?"

"None of your business."

"With who?" he says again, practically growling at me behind his wide smile.

My head snaps back. "Are you jealous?"

"Obviously." He leans in close, bending forward so our eyes are level, then strokes his finger down the length of my nose before booping me twice on the tip.

It's a gesture intended to piss me off, but it makes me want to cry because it's been so long since he last did it.

"So...?" he drawls.

"So?"

"So, are we going back to yours?"

"I just got here," I tell him.

Ryan stares at me, and I don't know why I'm trying to put off the inevitable. I came here for sex and the universe more than delivered. There's no point even trying to protest. I'm smiling. His eyes are twinkling. We're clearly picturing each other naked.

"Fine," I huff, my inner brat coming out to play. If I didn't love bickering with him so much, I'd have dragged him away five minutes ago. "Let's get out of here."

"My sister is here, and I brought a friend from L.A. with me. Let's say goodbye real quick."

I'm already tucked under his arm when he leads me away from the bar. We find Hannah at a table in the back corner, tucked between the wall and a guy with a cute mop of curls. They look like they're having a staring contest both are determined to win.

"Change of plans," Ryan tells them.

"Hi, Kayla," Hannah says, her cheeks turning red. I'd get in there and hug her if this gorgeous stranger she's clearly into wasn't in the way.

"It's good to see you."

"You here for the holidays?" she asks, hiding her blushes behind her almost empty beer. I hope Ryan wasn't supposed to be getting a round in when he found me at the bar.

"I live here full time now, actually. Started my touring business. Snow in the winter, bikes in the summer."

"That's fantastic," she says, but I care about Ryan's reaction more. He's the first person I ever shared my dream with, the only one who knows how much I wanted this.

A small thought pinches at my chest. I assumed their parents would have told them, since they definitely know all about it. Their Dad sent some boy band clients my way for mountain biking in the summer. Their TikTok videos kept me in business for the rest of the season.

I glance up at him and catch a look of pride on his face, but it's too much. He pulls me closer when I try to turn away, his arm dropping to my waist to squeeze me tight. New guy coughs, and Ryan snaps out of it.

"Kayla, this is my buddy Cameron." Cameron offers me his hand and I shake it as best I can while trapped in Ryan's hold.

"You joining us for a game?" he asks, deck of cards in his hand. I'm tempted. It's been too long since I whooped Ryan's ass at *L'Escalier*, and it's not polite to tell a man I just met that there's something more pressing on my mind.

I should make Ryan wait a little, work for it, but his hand has snuck under the back of my sweater and his thumb is stroking dangerously close to the clasp of my bra. I glare at him, willing him to be a little less obvious, and I'm about to accept Cameron's offer when he answers for me.

"We're gonna head off actually," he tells them, eyes never leaving mine. "I'll see you losers in the morning."

Ryan slips his fingers between mine, leading me through the packed crowd. The lights are dim, the music is loud, and it's only going to get busier from here.

"Do you have your sledge?" he asks me, picking up his old plastic one from a stash by the door. Our parents' houses are lower in the valley and it's a ritual to sledge home after drinks.

"Don't need one." I tell him, grabbing my jacket from the coat stand in the corner that threatens to topple any second. "My apartment isn't far."

"Since when do you have an apartment?"

"Since I moved here and only need a small space."

Besides the chalet we inherited from my grandmother, my parents own a few properties in this resort, but all were much too big for me.

February will mark a year since I made the move, so of course he doesn't know shit about where I live or what my life looks like now. He doesn't know how hard I've worked, or how many nights I've dreamed of the moment when I'd see him again.

Chapter 3
Ryan

So that's why her house was dark when I went over to surprise her last night. She's not even living there.

I guess a lot has changed since I saw her last, but not the way she bites her bottom lip when she looks at me. And definitely not the way my cock perked up as soon as I saw her walk in tonight.

I throw an arm around her shoulder and pull her closer while we walk. "I'm really proud of you, by the way. Your own touring business? You did it. All your dreams came true."

"Not all of them," she scoffs, jabbing me in the ribs with her pointy elbow. I yelp and rub the sore spot there.

"What's that supposed to mean?"

She shrugs and rolls her eyes. "How's Hollywood?"

"Work is work." I love my job, but I don't want to talk about it while I'm here with her.

"Cameron seems nice," she says. "What's his deal?"

"We work for the same studio, but then he's got this mad side gig that makes him loads of money. It was him who flew us both out."

"It's not foot stuff, is it?"

"I thought we weren't supposed to kink shame?" I tease. Kayla stops walking, cocks her head and gives me the same look I always get when she's had enough of my shit.

I give her the lowdown on Cameron's audio erotica alter-ego, *Mac'n'Please*, and hope to god she isn't one of his fans. I don't fully understand it all, but I know he records stories about his sexual exploits and puts them on the internet where thousands of women pay for the pleasure of listening to him moan.

I didn't think I could understand how people get turned on by just a voice, but hearing Kayla's Scottish accent again is proving me wrong.

"Oh, that's hot. He has a sexy voice."

I scoop a little snow from the roof of a car and flick it in her direction. "You heard him say five words in a noisy bar."

"So? I can tell. And you know how much I love dirty talk."

"Still as much as before?"

"Maybe," she says, storming off ahead of me. "Maybe more."

I've never met a woman with a mouth like Kayla's, in more ways than one. She might look like this sweet angel, all blonde hair, blue eyes and strong thighs built from miles on the mountain. Underneath it all, I know the real Kayla has a filthy side.

She wasn't lying when she said her apartment wasn't far. We round one corner, then another, then we're at her building. I follow her inside, dumping my sledge by the door and kneeling to unlace my boots. When she bends over to do the same to hers, I get a perfect view of her ass. Her boots stop mid-calf and take a lot longer to remove than mine, so I take full advantage and stand behind her, holding her hips to keep her steady.

"Where's your bedroom?"

"Don't you want the tour first?" she says, smacking my hand away. What I really want is to cup her hard between the legs.

"Not especially." She pulls her second boot off, then shoves me back against the wall.

I don't get it. She invited me back to her place, but she keeps pushing me away. Literally. Usually the talking comes later, but I'm in no rush if she needs to move at a slower pace this time.

"OK, fine, show me around."

It's the shortest tour in history. One corridor, two bedrooms on one side and a bathroom on the other.

"You live with someone?"

She shakes her head. "My office. It's mostly full of equipment, but it's nice to have a space if friends want to visit."

The rest of her house is open plan. It's not a flashy place like the chalets her parents own, but it's all Kayla. Soft blankets and cushions scattered on the sofa, a box of her favourite chocolate cereal on the counter that separates the kitchen and living room. A large sectional sofa takes up one corner of the room, facing a small TV and a bookcase spilling over with romance novels. I pick one up and recognise it's the same one my sister has had her nose buried in since we arrived.

On one wall, she's pinned a bunch of photographs. Pictures I recognise from spots we've been to together, a few I assume are with her friends from back home in Scotland. There's a cute one of her making cookies with her grandma when she was little. One with me carrying her on my back, her legs around my waist, snow in her hair. I forget who took it.

I pull back the long curtains to see what she can see from her window. The tops of other buildings lower down the mountain, twinkling lights and then darkness.

"Nice view."

"Mine's better," she says. Turning, I find her hopping up onto the counter across the kitchen, her crooked finger beckoning me. I make her wait, taking time to saunter over, stopping to fold my jacket and hoodie neatly over the back of one of her dining chairs.

I'm *dying* to kiss her. Don't know how I didn't drag her out of Rico's bar the second I laid eyes on her. Kayla is, hands down, the best kisser on the planet, and I know once I start I won't be able to stop.

She parts her thighs and I step in between them. It's been too fucking long, the longest we've gone without seeing each other, but standing this close, it feels like it's been no time at all.

She's still the same Kayla. Still wears three gold studs in each earlobe, and the dainty snowflake necklace that sits at the hollow of her throat. Her hair is still long, styled in thick braids she once trained me to weave for her. She still has the same sun-kissed freckles on her cheeks and her nose, the same full lips I'm going to take advantage of.

"Nice beard," she says, tipping her chin.

"You like it?"

"I like it."

Her eyes search mine for a few seconds and then she leans in, our noses brushing slowly from side to side. I pull back and she lets out a frustrated groan.

"I will headbutt you if you don't hurry up and kiss me."

I dart my tongue out to lick her lips, my fingertips tugging up her sweater, toying with the button on her jeans. I nudge it open and watch her eyes flare when I pull her zipper down ever so slowly.

"Lift your hips." She does, and I hook my fingers inside her clothing and tug hard. She gasps loudly when I pull it all off in one go, and toss it aside, leaving her naked from the waist down. My hands drift to the backs of her toned calves, stroking them up and down. Fuck, I've missed this body.

The scar on her shin I always trace with my thumb, evidence of the winter she took a nasty tumble, shredded her ski pants and twisted her ankle. We were thirteen years old. I chased the ski patrol stretcher all the way down the mountain, and refused to ski again until she could, too.

I squeeze just above her knees, then again and again, inching my way up her firm quads. She's always had an athletic body, but she must ski every day now she's here full time, and it shows in the taut muscles that twitch in response to my touch.

Kayla tries to push her knees back together, but I know it's all for show. I can see in her eyes how much she's aching for my touch. Know how wet I'll find her when my thumbs reach the top of her thighs and spread her aching flesh. I know every inch of this woman, because she's mine.

When she tries to push forward and grind against me, I grip her hips and hold her in place.

"You got a wishlist?"

"I didn't think you were coming, so I didn't see the point," she pouts.

"Hmm," I sigh softly, bending to press a kiss, an apology, to the top of her knee. "Mine's a mile long."

With only two weeks in the Alps each winter, three if we're lucky, we've gotten good at making the most of our time together. There's no wasting time on pleasantries and getting reacquainted. Instead, we used to arrive armed with lists in our heads. All the things we wanted to do, shit we only trusted each other with.

With hushed voices and hurried hands, Kayla and I have done a lot over the years, but always while sneaking away from our families. Now, in an apartment, with plenty of time and nobody to walk in on us, I don't even know where to begin.

"Ryan..." she whines, my thumbs stroking the softest lines just outside where her underwear would have been. Hearing her get needy and desperate is the best sound in the world, and I'm curious to see how far I can take it.

"What's up, Bunny?"

"Please, can you make me come?"

"I'll get you there. Let me play with it first." I push her ankles wider and lift them up to the lip of the kitchen counter. "Hold these up."

Chapter 4
Ryan

SHE DOES AS SHE'S told, and her head falls back against the cabinet above. I drop to my knees and watch my fingers spread her slickness from side to side, coating her folds.

Kayla McInnes has had the upper hand for as long as I've known her. She's a measly six weeks older than me and she loves to remind me every chance she gets. She learned to ski first, and she's always been faster. She was better at school, speaks better French, can light a better fire. And she's an assassin at card games who can drink me under the table any day of the week.

Still, when it comes to sex, I'd argue I'm better at making her lose her mind, and she doesn't have the advantage now. Not when I have her spread open and aching. I swipe my thumb over her clit, just as pretty as I remember, and she jerks at the sensation.

"Fuck, I missed this view. Best view on the planet."

She's trimmed her hair into a neat strip, smooth and glistening underneath. I've seen all her variations over the years, but this one makes me think she was hoping to get laid tonight. I can't tell whether that pisses me off or makes me even harder.

"Have you changed?"

She drops her head forward and stares down at me. "What?"

"Have you changed, or are you the same pretty little slut that likes me to remind her who her pussy belongs to?"

Inches from my face, she throbs again, and I take it as my answer.

"What'll it be, Kayla? Do you want a good boy or a bad boy?"

"Bad, so bad," she huffs out. I nip a chunk of thigh between my teeth and shake my head like a wolf with caught prey.

That's how it's always been with us. Two people with tastes that dance around the edge of what most people would deem socially acceptable. Whether we're up the mountain or sneaking around in our parents' houses, Kayla loves the thrill of the chase, the climb. The higher the risk, the greater the reward, as far as she's concerned.

I love to lure out the raw animal inside of her. To bite her and make her bite back. To taunt and tease, to trap her and make her mine. Love to make her ache and beg, and I've always, *always,* loved to play with my food.

Without warning, I thrust my tongue inside and feast like a starving man. I can't for the life of me remember what the fuck I've been doing all these years when I could have been doing this.

Her hips tilt forward, driving against my mouth. She lets go of one ankle, draping it over my shoulder so her fingers can sink into my hair. Her moan matches mine when she grips the strands at the back and pulls me in closer. It's a small claim for power, but there's no way I'm giving it up just yet.

I shift my focus to her clit, nudging it from side to side, applying the lightest pressure with my tongue. Her deep moans shift to needy whimpers, and my dick gets painfully hard in my jeans. Pulling back, I watch myself slide two fingers in to the hilt, then drag them in and out of her, deep and slow and first, then harder and faster.

Looking up, I catch her watching too, and when our eyes lock, I pull them out and take my time to suck them clean.

"You want a taste?" I ask, and she nods, her mouth falling open. She's so fucking wet, there's plenty for both of us. I push them inside her again, extra deep, then stand up and paint her mouth with it.

Palm up, I offer her my fingers, then at the last second bend my middle one to my mouth so she can suck one while I suck the other. Her tongue is magnificent, swirling its way down until it meets mine, and I pull my hand away and kiss her like my life depends on it.

She opens for me, letting me lick into her mouth, and the taste of her pussy on her own tongue drives me insane. I can't stop, but I need to get her off, fast.

I squeeze her tits through her sweater, then trail my hand down to roam between her spread thighs. Once my fingers stroke deep, I trace circles around her clit and relish the sound of her moaning into my mouth. Her other foot slips off the edge of the counter and I pick it back up and plant it wider.

Our kisses are sloppy and desperate. She nips me with her teeth, and I nip her back. Her nails dig into my neck and my free hand grips one of her braids, yanking her head to the side so I can moan in her ear, just the way she likes.

"Need you to come on my hand, Bunny. Show me what I've been missing."

I add pressure in the right spot , then Kayla McInnes, the most beautiful girl in the world, shatters in front of me. I watch her face, her eyes squeezed tightly, head tipped back, mouth open and gasping for air as her hips jerk roughly.

She always gets super sensitive after she comes, but I've missed out on so much time with her, I can't stop now. I drop to my knees and work her clit with my tongue again, not letting up even while she whimpers and whines, squirming on the countertop. I can't tell if she's pulling me closer or pushing me away, but with my tongue flicking from side to side, it's not long before she comes again, clamping her shaking thighs around my head.

When she's ready to cut me loose, I stand and lick a hot wet stripe up the column of her throat.

"Missed you so fucking much," I tell her, but she barely pauses to catch her breath before hopping off the counter and switching places with me. I worry about her knees on the hard tile, but then she's pulling my clothes down, wrapping her pretty lips around the head of my cock, and I'm seeing stars.

"Jesus, fuck, Kayla, give me a second to—" I pull my t-shirt off and drop it on the floor.

"No," she moans around it, sliding her wet mouth further down my shaft, nudging me towards the back of her throat. I used to worry about making her gag until she told me how much she loved it, too. She bobs her head, coating my length with spit, then wrapping her hand around it, stroking me firmly.

I keep my eyes on her mouth, scooping a braid in each fist while she works me over, swirling her tongue around the throbbing head.

"Can I see your tits?" I plead. She yanks her top up, puffs her chest out to keep it lifted, then gets back to smacking my dick against her flattened tongue. A strangled moan rumbles out of me. This view should be illegal.

One downside of our arrangement is that I never see photos of her. It's also a positive, because if she ever graced me with a photo of her tits, I'd get no work done, and I'd turn into an even bigger menace and start begging for new ones every day.

Whenever I think about her in a sexual way, which is far more than I should, it's usually like this. On her knees, greedy, worshipping. She once bet she could make me come in under a minute without using her hands, then shaved thirteen seconds off the target.

She's the benchmark, the blueprint, and if she wanted to tattoo her signature along the side of it, I'd let her and say thank you. That's how much she owns my dick. Everything it knows, it learned from her, everything it likes, it's all because of her.

I couldn't hold off even if I wanted to.

"I'm close. I'm gonna—" I grip those braids tighter, the only thing keeping me from crumbling to the floor. "Where do you want—"

Kayla grabs my ass, short, sharp nails digging in as she pulls me deeper into her mouth. I look down at my pretty girl, this beautiful mess, eyes wide, mouth sloppy with drool spilling out at the sides. Something in my chest pinches, then snaps, and my orgasm roars forth, flooding her mouth as her cheeks hollow out. My hips buck with each release, moans filling the room.

I stroke her cheeks with my thumbs until she deigns to release me from her heavenly grip. She smiles up at me, panting, proud, and satisfied, as she swallows me down. One final white stream spurts out of me, landing on the sweater bunched at her throat.

This is bad form. I should have taken the time to get her naked. It's the least she deserved. It's not the fastest we've gotten each other off at the start of a trip. I think the last time I visited, I was inside her before we'd even said hello. Tonight might be the best, though, outstripping anything my brain came up with in our years apart. I swipe a drop of cum from the corner of her lips with my thumb, then lick it off.

Kayla hops to her feet and fixes her clothes back into place. I'm about to pull her into my arms, but some cloud descends. Her mouth presses into a tight pout, head shaking as our eyes lock.

"You fucking bastard."

Chapter 5

Kayla

One Winter Ago / Age Twenty-Seven

The look on Cheryl's face tells me everything I wish I wasn't dying to know.

He's not here, and he's not coming.

It was stupid of me to assume he would definitely come home after missing last year. When she opens her arms to hug me, I force a tight smile and will myself not to let her see me shed tears over her son.

"Ryan sends his love," she whispers, stroking my back for a long time. They're just words. And they don't mean shit.

Chapter 6
Kayla

Wiping my mouth with the back of my hand, I shove Ryan hard against his chest. With his jeans still around his knees, he topples backwards and lands on his ass.

"What's wrong?"

"Three years, Ryan! You skip two winters and not so much as a phone call?"

"Who makes phone calls?" he laughs, and I want to scream.

"A text, an email, a DM. A fucking postcard would have been nice, but nothing? Nothing is..."

Agony. It's been agony.

"It's insulting," I settle on, then storm off to the bathroom. After cleaning myself up, I take a long hard look in the mirror. I don't know whether I'm mad at him or myself. I thought I was doing a stellar job of getting over him, and all it took was one second in his presence to fall right back in.

Now he's scrambling my brain with orgasms - *multiple, the bastard* - and I don't know what to think. My heart is still racing, every nerve alive and humming. If he led me to bed, I'm not sure we'd ever get out of it.

Nobody does it like Ryan Richmond, because nobody's ever stuck around long enough to learn what I really like.

Except, that's not entirely accurate. I don't let anyone stick around, don't let people in. I put someone over him once, and it was the most miserable winter and a total waste of time. After that, I kept men at arm's length, until I gave up waiting. Ryan had clearly given up on me, or so I thought.

In my bedroom, I strip out of the clothes he's made a mess of, and curse my stupid, horny, touch-starved brain for bringing him back here. Memories of him are everywhere on this mountain, but this apartment has been a place just for me. It will be impossible to ignore thoughts of him now I've watched him eat me out in the exact spot where I make my morning coffee.

"Are you *not* happy to see me?" he smirks, leaning against my door frame, still topless and gorgeous. God he looks good with a tan. "Because you looked pretty happy coming on my tongue five minutes ago."

His gaze heats my skin as it travels from my legs to my hips and settles there. I'd slam the door in his face, but it's nothing he hasn't seen before. I pull on soft sleep shorts and a worn t-shirt from a ski racing contest I volunteered at during my first season here.

"I saw your parents in the *boulangerie* three days ago, and they said you weren't coming home." He doesn't need to know I came home and cried myself to sleep, thinking he'd forgotten all about me. My pillow is probably still stained with tears.

"I didn't know I was coming until right before our flight. It was a totally last minute decision."

Ryan spins me some story about him and Cameron getting drunk and booking tickets on a whim, which does nothing to reassure me he genuinely wants to be here. He didn't come here for me. He hasn't ached the way I've ached for him.

"I haven't heard from you. In years."

"Doesn't mean I haven't thought about you every day."

My head almost spins off my shoulders. I could actually throttle him. "Have you? Because that would have been nice to know."

His face sinks, and it's in this moment I see him understand this is no joke to me.

"But we agreed, didn't we? Not to get involved with each other's lives while we were apart. You do your thing, I do mine, and then it's, you know... *'see you next winter'*."

That pact was the stupidest mess I've ever gotten myself into.

"Our agreement didn't include disappearing off the face of the earth."

"I didn't disappear! I was in L.A."

Tugging the ends of my braids free, I loosen them and brush them out with less of the delicate care I usually give my hair.

"Oh, don't worry, I know all about your fancy Hollywood life and what you've been up to because I still see your parents every year. I get to sit there with a smile on my face, pretending I don't miss you while they tell me what show you're working on and all about your beautiful new girlfriend."

"What girlfriend?"

"The redhead!"

He laughs and shakes his head. "She's not my girlfriend anymore."

"Since when? And don't you dare say you just broke up because if you make me feel like a rebound, I will kick you in the dick."

"Since February. It was a really brief thing. She got a modelling contract in New York."

"A model?" I screech, throwing my hands in the air and shoving past him. "Well, that's brilliant, isn't it? Golden boy with his cool friends and his supermodel girlfriend coming back to fuck my life up."

"We're not even in touch," he calls after me.

It used to be so easy when we were kids. We'd say goodbye, then live our separate lives, me in Scotland, him in London. He was just a friend I saw on holiday, and while it was a comfort knowing we'd be reunited the following winter, I never really missed him.

Obviously kissing complicated things, sex even more so, and somewhere along the line we decided this would be our own tradition. A *'what happens in the mountains, stays in the mountains'* agreement that was clearly easier for him than it's been for me.

"What is this all about, Kayla?" he asks, following me into the living room where I busy myself with straightening the sofa cushions and blankets. I hadn't been expecting guests. Least of all him.

It's been a busy week, and I've not kept on top of tidying. Though he's been in my bedroom at my parents' house plenty of times, I don't want him judging me or the home I've built for myself.

"Oh shit, are you with someone?" he asks, and the cushion hits him square in the chest before my brain even registers I've chucked it.

"Do you think I'd have let you come in my mouth if I was with someone, Ryan?" I shriek, catching it when he throws it back. "Argh, you are so infuriating!"

"Have you been with anyone else?"

My jaw drops. That was not part of the deal. Our entire... whatever we are, only works on the understanding we don't talk about whatever we get up to when we're not in the mountains. We turn up, fuck as much as feasibly possible, and off we go. Him asking means he gives a shit, and I can't have him dropping bombs like that when I've convinced myself he doesn't.

"You're not supposed to ask," I say, turning away to pick up the empty cereal bowl I left on my coffee table this morning.

"Well, I'm asking."

"This is the first time I've seen you in three years, so I think it would be pretty rude of you to expect me not to sleep with anyone else."

"That's fair." He tries to touch my arm when I pass him, but I duck out of reach and the spoon goes clattering across the kitchen floor. I squat to pick it up and when I look at him, all I see is heat in his eyes.

"Don't you stand there half-naked and hot and give me that look." I pick his t-shirt up off the kitchen floor and throw it at him. He's not quick enough, and when it lands on his face, I pinch my lips together to hide my satisfied smile. "Put your clothes on before you talk to me in my house."

He grabs the rest of his things and disappears to clean himself up. I pull a pan from the cupboard and click on the stovetop to warm milk. Once little bubbles appear on the surface, I add two scoops of chocolate flakes and stir them slowly with my grandma's old wooden spoon.

Ryan has the sense to keep his mouth shut when he gets back, pulling out a stool to sit at my breakfast bar. I focus on the dull scrape of the spoon against the bottom of the pan, making sure the milk doesn't catch. When all the chocolate has melted, I pour the rich liquid into two mugs and carry them over to where he waits, watching. My place isn't big, and there's no option but to hop up onto the other stool.

"So you missed me?" he says.

"Of course I missed you, but I'm still mad as hell."

"I like you mad." He ducks his head to nip at my jaw. "Makes me want to put you over my knee."

My core clenches at the thought. He's very good at spanking, always takes his time to really draw it out and tease me until I'm a begging mess. Whenever I've asked someone else to do it, it hasn't been nearly as good.

"Did you miss me?" I ask him and immediately wish I hadn't. I shouldn't care, and this is only going to end badly.

"Are you kidding me? Winters are nothing without you. Winters aren't even winter in California."

"How long are you here for?"

"We fly home January 3rd."

Almost two weeks. Two weeks I've crammed with ski tour bookings, so I wouldn't have to spend my time pining over him.

"I have a lot of work on," I tell him.

"So squeeze me in whenever you can."

I ignore him and lose myself in my hot chocolate instead. There'll be pockets of time, but if he wants them, he'll have to grovel.

"Come on, you know I'll make it so good for you," he says, reading my mind. "We have a lot of time to make up for, and I'll do whatever shit you've been dreaming up, nasty girl."

I nearly choke on my drink and slam my mug down on the counter. "Don't shame me!"

"Hey, hey," he says, twisting me to lift my legs into his lap. I almost topple backwards and grab his arm to steady myself. "I would never, ever shame you. You know I think you're the hottest thing I've ever seen. It's an honour to fuck you."

"Damn right it is. Now get out of here before I change my mind."

I climb down and snatch up our mugs, not caring he's only had half of his hot chocolate. He watches me tip both down the sink and looks at me like I'm insane, but I hold my ground and point to the door.

"Out."

"I can't stay over?"

"Absolutely not. That was the deal. No sleepovers, no one gets caught."

"But I've stayed over before? And there's nobody here." He has a point, but everything is different now. The last time he stayed over, he walked out of my life.

I can't get it straight in my head, and I need some time to think without him crowding my home and my thoughts.

He closes the space between us with caution, carefully reaching for my hands. The gentle touch of him slipping his fingers between mine.

"Kayla, everyone knows about us. They have for years."

"It's different now. I live here full time, I work here, I have a life. Please allow me the dignity of not looking like I fell straight back in with you because you deigned to grace us with your presence this Christmas."

With all my might, I shove him down the hallway to my front door, grab his jacket from the hook, and press it into his hands.

"Besides, I have a touring gig at ten and if you stay over, I know you'll keep me up all night."

"But what about the pact? We agreed—" I pinch his lips between my thumb and forefinger before he can say another word.

"I know what we agreed, but you're fucking with my head, and you need to go." I can feel his tongue trying to push out and lick me and I want to laugh so hard, the way only this particular idiot ever makes me laugh.

With my other hand, I open the door and barge him over the threshold. He shoves back, hooking one ankle around my leg and trying to pull him with me. His easy laugh tumbles out of him, and I've missed it so much I almost stop. Flirting with him is always so playful and fun.

God, it would be so easy to switch tactics and push him in the other direction. A little naked wrestling in my bedroom wouldn't be a bad way to burn off this nervous energy that is one hundred percent his fault.

He hip-checks me, his hands trying to loosen my grip on his waist, but I'll never let him win this one. Thanks to my days spent cruising the mountain, I'm in the best physical shape of my life. He might be taller and wider than me, but California and a desk job have made him soft.

I extend my leg behind me to kick his boots, one, then the other, through the door and down the hallway. One teeters on the lip of the stairs then topples over the edge, drawing his attention long enough for me to slam the door behind him.

Breathless, I rest my back against it, wondering what the fuck I'm playing at. I've never wanted anything more than I want him, and I'm thrilled he's here. So why am I sending him away?

"I'm coming to see you before you head up the mountain," he yells from the other side of the door.

"Don't promise me shit," I yell back.

"I'll be there, Bunny. I swear."

Chapter 7

Ryan

Two Winters Ago / Age Twenty-Six

My weekly calls for Hannah started as a need for proof of life when a break-up sent her spiraling, but now she's the one who chases me.

"Mum and Dad will be so disappointed," she says.

"I know, and I'll tell them I'm sorry, OK?"

"You really can't get away?"

"No, this film is really behind schedule. There's no shooting over the holidays, but sound mixing can go ahead. I can't be the reason it gets delayed any longer."

She sighs and sips her tea. "OK, I get it. I'll probably be the same once I qualify. I'm just sad about it, that's all. It won't be the same without you."

"I'll be there next year, I promise."

"What about Kayla?" she says.

"What about her?"

"Ryan!" she scolds, and I feel exactly as ashamed as I should. This is a shitty move on my part, but I know it's the right call.

"Can you tell her I'm sorry and I'll see her next winter?"

"No way. You can tell her yourself," Hannah says, hanging up before I can admit I don't even have a way to contact Kayla.

Chapter 8
Ryan

CROWDS GATHER AT THE bottom of the *Express Telecabin* each morning, and it's everyone for themselves as they queue for lift passes, lessons, and a spot on the first ascent. This lift is popular for good reason. It's the quickest way to the top of the mountain where you can access slopes of all levels and work your way into the other valleys.

Kayla had already left her apartment by the time I knocked with fresh pastries, and if I don't find her here, then I'll have broken my promise.

I wasn't sure how my return would make her feel, and last night was hot and confusing. We haven't lost our spark after all these years apart, and when I found out she has her own place, I thought she'd let me stay the night and take advantage of uninterrupted time together. Clearly, I've got some work to do to make it up to her.

Finally, I spot her in the crowd, her bright pink helmet like a beacon in a sea of dark ones.

"Kayla!" I call out, weaving my way, ducking to avoid a head injury from those who carry their skis horizontally. "*Excusez-moi, excusez-moi.*"

She says something to the group she's with, and storms towards me. "What are you doing here?"

"I said I'd see you before your lessons. I brought you breakfast."

"I ate hours ago," she says, but takes the paper bag anyway, tugging her rucksack round to one side and shoving it inside. "I'm with clients."

"Can you meet for lunch? We're going to The Marmot."

In France, families celebrate Christmas on December twenty-fourth, but we have plenty of our own family traditions. On the twenty-third we have lunch at *The Marmot*, the highest restaurant on the mountain. Steaming, glutenous bowls of French onion soup followed by whatever the daily special is. Hannah and I are partial to a slice of mandarin cheesecake, too.

Afterwards, we race each other home, then Hannah and Dad do the Christmas food shop while Mum and I chill in the hot tub or watch a movie. Kayla has always been a welcome addition to our family festivities, and it's cool to have Cam with us, too.

"I'll be in the other valley."

"Well, what about later?"

"My parents are arriving today."

"Then when can I see you?" I grab the sleeve of her ski jacket, and she swats my hand away, lowering her voice.

"I'll see you when I see you, Ryan. You can't expect me to drop everything just because you showed up and you're horny."

Fuck.

That's exactly how this looks, and I hate myself for it.

"That is not why I want to see you." She fixes me with a stare and her pretty pout. "Not the *only* reason I want to see you. I missed you, and I want to ski with you."

"You want to ski with me?"

"Oh yeah," I say, pushing my luck by pressing a kiss to her cheek. "I think this is the year I'll finally beat you in our race to the bottom."

"After three years off? I highly doubt it."

She storms off and guides her tour group through the ticket gates and onto the packed lift. In under a minute, it leaves the station, and I'm still here wondering how I'm supposed to make this right with her.

Chapter 9
Kayla

Today was a dream day. Bright bluebird skies, fun clients, perfect snow conditions. The beer they bought me after our last run was crisp, and they left me with a hefty tip and a promise they'll book me again next year.

To top it all off, I got an hour in my parents' hot tub with a spicy book after they arrived armed with supplies for dinner. Mum whipped up a light meal of salads and charcuterie, all we need ahead of a few days of feasting, and we've caught up while eating. Though I only see them a few times a year, we video chat a lot, so it doesn't feel like five months since they were last here.

Both my family and Ryan's family were lucky to inherit mountain properties, and though they're listed as year round holiday rentals, we've always kept the Christmas weeks for ourselves.

Mum's mum was French, and though she later lived in Scotland, she kept the house, insisting her children and grandchildren would enjoy holidays on the mountain as she had as a girl. Our grandmothers were best friends, and our parents spent winters here long before Ryan and I were even born.

It's been a long time since they passed, but they live on in our memories and traditions.

My parent's chalet has been improved and extended since then, with a second balcony added to the top floor, a rear terrace with a hot tub, and two additional bedrooms downstairs making it a perfect destination for families. It's much too big for us three, but it's beautiful and rustic, full of authentic alpine charm and holds a special place in my heart.

In the daytime, our views of the mountain are unmatched, and on a clear evening, you can see further down into the valley and all the little villages twinkling below.

I've never known peace or happiness like the feeling I get in this house. I haven't stayed here since last Christmas, though. It was always a home from home when I lived in Scotland, but I have my apartment in the next village now, so I'll probably only stay here for a few nights of their visit. It makes more sense to wake up closer to where I meet my clients each morning.

I know the night could get even better if I swing past Ryan's house. It would be so easy. All I have to do is put my shoes on and coat on, walk four houses up the lane, and knock on the door.

His parents would welcome me in. We'd make knowing eyes at each other across the room, and I'd kick his ass over cards, but I will not let myself do any of that. It was sweet of him to bring me food this morning, but there is no way I am chasing him for a second of his time. If he wants me, he knows where to find me.

"We saw Cheryl and Mark as we were arriving," Dad says, topping up my glass with a healthy slug of Beaujolais. "They said Ryan's home this year."

My back stiffens. I know exactly where this is going. "Yep, saw him yesterday."

"That's exciting, isn't it?"

"Is it?" I shove another piece of bread in my mouth.

"The whole gang's back together," Mum chimes in.

"What gang?"

"You three kids. Just like old times."

I can feel my cheeks turning pink, and it's not from the heat of the roaring fire we light most days. They're probably referring to all the times we spent together as children, not the more recent times where Ryan and I played a few strictly after hours games of our own.

As kids, I'd invite him and Hannah round for board games and movies, or we'd go for late night walks with our grandmothers to see the lights in the village. At some point, those nights got later and later. We'd sneak kisses on the doorstep, or say goodnight when our families headed to bed, then fool around on the sofa until it was time to drag ourselves apart.

"It's different now," I tell them, hoping they'll leave it alone. "And anyway, he has a friend with him."

"A *female* friend?" Mum gasps.

"No, some American guy he lives with. Cameron."

"Well, you already look happier than last year," Dad says, squeezing my shoulder.

Ah yes, last year where I spent every minute I wasn't skiing moping on their sofa, eating chocolate coins, and crying all over the mountain. Hannah and I met up to ski one morning, but I spent the entire time trying to work up the courage to ask for her brother's phone number, then hating myself for being so desperate.

"You should not be encouraging this."

"We're just saying it's nice you're all here, darling," Mum says. "That's all."

My friends back in Edinburgh would say I'm lucky my parents aren't putting any pressure on me to find a man and settle down. As we approach our thirties, all of them are being asked when grandchildren might be on the cards, as if kids are the ultimate ticket to happiness.

It's not that I don't want kids, but I don't let my thoughts go there. I've spent so many years hankering after my next fix of Ryan, I never stopped to think about what our arrangement meant for my long-term relationship prospects. Obviously, it's not going to be him, but his hold on me means I've struggled to give anyone else a real chance.

There's an endless supply of hot guys out here, and most are on vacation or working a season. I've always viewed them as an opportunity for some no-strings fun, something to scratch an itch.

Thanks for the sex, see you never.

Meeting someone who lives here year round is much more terrifying. It's not a big town, and I couldn't bear the awkwardness of dating someone, then having to see them around when it inevitably went wrong.

And it would. I'd make it go wrong because, despite my attempts to get over him, I'm still a silly little girl with a crush on Ryan Richmond. No man has ever come close to the way he makes me feel.

These years apart have been an emotional rollercoaster that has seen me crying, pining, and cursing his name in equal measure.

I've tried to pretend he's dead to me, but it's impossible. Sometimes when I ski past a spot that holds strong memories, I wonder if I moved here permanently to be closer to him in spirit, if not geographically. I cruise around the slopes, haunted by the memory of his bright laugh and warm hugs. It's not fair he's so good in bed *and* the best hugger.

I know there are two people in this… whatever this is. I could probably have tracked him down any time, but after the first Christmas where he didn't come home, every month made it harder to get in touch.

What if he wasn't bothered? What if he texted back *'who is this?'* and it wasn't a joke? I'd never recover.

I'm not going to be caught dead hunting down a man to ask if he would please grace me with his presence for two measly weeks of the year. Trying to move on from him is a constant work in progress, and if he hadn't shown his face this year, I don't know if I'd ever have been able to give him another.

How long am I supposed to wait for scraps of nothing?

Chapter 10
Ryan
Three Winters Ago / Age Twenty-Five

Our situation is no secret, and I think our families know we find it tough to say goodbye to each other. In the last days of our visit, they give us space to be alone, which is how I've found myself sat across from Kayla in her parents' hot tub. Her head rests against the edge, bubbles breaking all over the front of her chest, and I spy a red bruise from where I sucked too hard on her skin.

I'm happy to be leaving her with a mark even though I know it will fade not long after I'm gone.

"Our last night," I sigh. "Is there anything we didn't get around to doing?"

She shakes her head, a sleepy, satisfied smile on her face. "I think this was our best year yet, you know? We ticked everything off."

Kayla brought a few new toys to experiment with, a strawberry lube we both agreed we taste way better without. Last night, on her request, I snuck into her bedroom from the balcony and covered her mouth while I edged her with my fingers.

My list wasn't very long. After so many years of not sleeping over, all I wanted was to wake up with her and have sleepy morning sex, just like I long for back home in my new L.A. apartment. We threw out the rulebook last night, and fell asleep in each other's arms. I woke up with her hand in my pants, then her mouth making all my wishes come true.

"I'm glad I make all your dreams come true."

Beneath the water, she kicks her foot out, but I grab it with both hands and press my thumbs into the sole. "You're so cheesy."

"Yeah, but you still love me."

It comes out of nowhere. My thumb stills and our eyes lock. We've never said that word to each other, barely spoken about our feelings at all. What's the point when we know we're saying goodbye so quickly?

"Oh, Ryan," she sighs, crossing the tub to slip into my lap. "I probably could love you, unfortunately."

"Why unfortunately?"

She rests her head on my shoulder, weaving her fingers through mine. Our fingertips line up and we press them into each other.

"I can't imagine anything worse than being miles away from the man I love."

Noted. Loud and clear.

My flight leaves a day earlier than hers, so I stay over and milk every minute, her words spinning over and over in my head.

This thing I have with Kayla, I can't imagine it with anyone else, but she's right. We live on opposite sides of the world. Two lives in two continents.

She falls asleep around three, her head on my chest, knee hooked up and over my hip. It's not comfortable, and I barely sleep, but I don't give a shit. I want every single second with her. I stroke my fingers through her hair, count her eyelashes, and wonder if one day we'll come here with children who look half like me and half like her.

When I know I can't drag it out any longer, I roll her onto her side, slip out of bed, and pull my clothes on.

"I'll see you next winter, Bunny."

"See you next winter," she mumbles, pulling my pillow to her chest and curling herself around it. The covers shift enough to reveal the bumps of her spine and the curve of her ass. I drop a kiss on one perfect, round cheek, then cover her up.

Later, I'll wish I'd taken a photo. This will be the image that haunts me when I decide to let her go.

Chapter 11
Ryan

December twenty-fourth is the main event here, and I've always loved how my family extends the festivities, by blending Christmas Eve and Christmas Day into one long celebration of food and relaxation.

After a day of stuffing our faces and hanging out in the hot tub, we bundle up to walk down to the town square for the traditional parade.

Having spent the last two holidays in sunny California, I've missed the way the local community shows up to celebrate the occasion. Since long before we were kids, crowds have gathered to see *Père Noël* as he travels through the town in his sleigh. For years I thought it was the real thing, but without kid goggles, it's clearly a man on the back of a truck with not a reindeer in sight.

Still, the streets are full of excited faces tipped up to admire the lights and unique displays in all the shop windows. Mum keeps stopping to show them all to Cameron, but when Hannah leads him off to buy roasted chestnuts, I look for Kayla.

It doesn't take long to track her down in one of our favourite spots, perched on the edge of the monument near the tourist office.

When I offer her my hand, she glances at it for a second, then pretends she hasn't seen me.

"Kayla," I growl up at her.

"I'm watching the parade," she says, shoving her hands under her thighs and out of my reach. "I have the best view from here."

"You'll have a better view if you come wriggle your way up front with me, like always."

She throws her head back and makes a sound that's half laughter, half groaning. "*'Like always'* implies you're always here, and that is blatantly not true."

"Well, I'm here now." Still, she doesn't budge. "Fine, scoot over and make space for me."

While attempting to boost myself up and sit next to her, I discover my fully grown ass is the same size as two kid ones and end up shoving her off the edge.

"Ryan, what the fuck?" she snaps, wincing when a nearby family turn to tut at her language.

Kayla turns her back on me, and I hop down again and throw my arms around her shoulders. She's the perfect height to rest my chin on her head.

"Are you still mad at me?"

"Yes," she huffs, but I can already feel her softening against my chest.

We've never been the kind of friends who argue, at least not about serious stuff. She might have lost her shit a couple of times when I've beaten her in a race to the bottom of the ski slope. Then there was the one time I was a selfish prick to her all winter break, but I did my best to make up for it the following year.

She lets me slip my gloved fingers between hers and lead her closer to the front of the parade where our parents are watching with Hannah and Cameron. She's been teaching him to ski this week, and it's cool to see my sister and my friend getting on so well. Makes me think I should invite her out to California sometime, if she can drag herself away from work.

It's not long before Santa rolls past, a convincing vision in red velvet and a full, bushy beard. His team of elves slip chocolate coins into the hands of the smallest children at the front, extra ones straight into pockets to make them feel special.

Dad takes photos of us all and pulls Cameron and Kayla in like they're part of the family. In many ways she is, but there are no photos of her in my house, so I make a mental note to ask Dad to send me these. There are a few old selfies buried in a hidden folder on my phone, but after seeing the ones on display in her apartment, it would be nice to print them out and frame them, too.

Christmas wouldn't be the same if she wasn't here to share it with, but that makes me feel like a fucking asshole. As it should. If I turned up at our house and she was a no-show, I'd be devastated. She's always been as sure a bet as the mountains themselves.

My grip on her hand tightens like maybe if I squeeze hard enough, she'll stay attached to me forever. What the fuck was I thinking skipping out on the past two winters? And what kind of asshole assumes a woman like Kayla would wait around for him? No wonder she was pissed as hell at seeing me.

To the untrained eye, you'd think she gives more of a shit about me than I do about her, but that couldn't be further from the truth.

Kayla has some cellular level effect on me. I swear I've heard her laughter carried on the wind, felt her phantom touch in those liminal moments before I wake up.

In the bedroom, we've basically trained each other. She's the only woman I ever think of when I come. The images that flash through my mind are a sensational stimulant when I'm alone, a colossal inconvenience when I've tried to get with anyone else.

"Do you have plans after dinner?" I ask her.

"Early night, I think," she says, looking down at her feet. Clearly I'm not invited, and I'm not happy about it.

"Can I see you?"

She pulls away and drops my hand. "I'm leading a Christmas sunrise tour tomorrow, so I need a good night's sleep."

One thing she definitely won't get with me in her bed.

"We're not skiing together?" I ask, trying not to look too disappointed. She's woven into all of my favourite holiday traditions. This parade, our annual Christmas morning race, the fireworks on New Year's Eve.

"It's work, Ryan. I can't drop clients."

"Can I meet you after?"

She inhales deeply and presses her lips together. "I don't know."

These stilted conversations are agony. We've always been so open with each other, and I wish I knew the magic words to fix things between us. The thought of this winter slipping away because we're in a fight I never meant to cause is unbearable.

Every part of me wants to scoop her up, throw her over my shoulder and haul her ass home, but I don't want to make things worse with her.

"Kayla. Bunny. Look at me." I pull my glove off and she lets me cup her face, tilting her head to lean into my warm touch. "I'm here. Right now. And if you don't want to see me then, well, that fucking sucks, but I'll deal with it. Somehow. If you do want to see me, and you're just protecting your heart, then I hate to pressure you, but I don't want to waste a single second we could be together."

Her pout lifts at one corner before she bites it back down. Surrounded by people, our families included, I know this isn't the time or the place for a grand declaration of my true feelings. Still, I need her to know how I feel, and it's the realest I can be for now.

"You know where I'll be. Any time you want to see me, even if it's for five minutes, I'm all yours."

"Tomorrow," she says, so softly I think I might have imagined it.

"Tomorrow?"

"I'll be skiing with my parents in the afternoon, but you can come to my apartment later."

"Seriously?"

It's like a light flicks on in my head, and I see it reflected in her eyes. Visions of me and her, alone at her place, hours stretched out before us. My wishlist is doubling in size, and she knows it.

She plants her hands on my chest and pushes me away, walking backwards. "Don't push your luck."

"You're the best, Bunny," I call after her as she slips her way through the crowd. "I—I'll see you tomorrow."

Fortunately, I catch myself before I tell her I love her, but it doesn't mean I don't feel it.

Chapter 12
Kayla
Five Winters Ago / Age Twenty-Three

IT'S THE FIRST DAY of winter break and even though I'm dying to get my hands on him, I've made Ryan chase me down the mountain all morning.

But now? Now I have him all to myself behind a hidden snowbank. We can't do anything here, but that doesn't mean we can't talk about it, and nothing turns me on like making dirty plans with Ryan.

He breaks our kiss and asks me first. "What's on your wishlist this year?"

"I want you to blindfold me."

"Deal. I want to get sucked off on a chairlift."

"What the fuck? How?"

"One of those bubble ones on the far side of the mountain. Takes seven mins to reach the top of the run. Think you could manage?"

"You know I could."

"What else?"

"I want you to rip my underwear sometime. Like, literally, tear them off me."

"Easy, no problem. I'll—"

"No, surprise me. And then shove them in my mouth while you fuck me."

He gasps and I get a sick thrill knowing I've shocked him. "Kayla, that's nasty shit. You're fucking filthy, but I'm so down."

"Yeah?"

"Abso-fucking-lutey. Kiss me again."

Chapter 13
Ryan

My family spend Christmas day mostly horizontal around the house, eating leftovers, playing games, reading and falling asleep in front of the television.

In the evening, Hannah heads to bed early with her books and a stash of chocolate, and Cameron and I play cards with my folks until the fire burns out.

"Have you enjoyed your first French Christmas, Cameron?" my mum asks, stifling a yawn.

He rubs his belly and catches her yawn. "A little too much, I think."

I know how he feels. The third slice of chocolate yule log was entirely unnecessary.

"Well, that's what Christmas in the mountains is all about," Mum says.

"Seriously though, it's been incredible. I can't thank you enough for your hospitality."

"You're very welcome, son," Dad says, giving him a squeeze on the shoulder. My parents have always accepted our friends with open arms, and Cameron is no different. This spontaneous trip could have been awkward if they weren't happy about him joining me, or if he didn't enjoy his time with us.

"Don't stay up too late, boys." Mum says on her way up the stairs. "Back on the slopes tomorrow."

The fire crackles and Cameron yawns again, his head tipped back against the armrest on the sofa. "I have a feeling this will be the best sleep of my life. You coming up?"

"I'm gonna nip out and see Kayla, actually."

"Oh, yeah?" he says, wiggling his eyebrows suggestively. "What's the deal with you two, anyway?"

"We're just friends," I tell him, my default answer.

"With benefits?"

"Something like that."

He gets up to follow me down the stairs that lead to the boot room and out of the house. "How come you've never mentioned her before?"

"I don't know, man." How do you explain a woman like Kayla, or our situation? "We've known each other since we were kids. At some point it became something else, but it's just a holiday hook-up thing."

"Do you like her more than that?"

"Sure, she's great." I pull on my coat and my boots. "But it's never going to be *more*. We both know that."

"Doesn't sound very convincing, bro."

"It's casual. Don't worry about it."

"If you say so."

"The dude who's fucked hundreds of women is a relationship expert now?"

"Oh my god," he groans. "For the millionth time, my audios *simulate* sex. I'm not actually recording it."

I don't know how he makes his content, and don't want to know, but I love to wind him up about it.

"You cool if I head back later in the morning? Hannah will be here if you need anything."

"It's all good, man. I can keep myself entertained. Have a fun night."

Outside, soft flakes sweep through the air, but for now the road is still clear enough to drive the five minutes up the hill to the next village where Kayla lives. Normally I'd ride the chairlift that connects the two villages to head up there for dinner or drinks at Rico's, but it's late and it stopped running hours ago.

This after-hours rendezvous would be easier if she were staying with her parents a few houses down the road, but I love the idea of alone time in her apartment. Dad won't mind if I take the car from the garage and bring it back in the morning, but even if he did, I'd find a way to get to her.

We're no strangers to sneaking around. I've lost count of the number of times I climbed up to the balcony outside her bedroom window after everyone was asleep. It was risky, but we both loved the thrill.

The roads are so quiet, I pull up outside her house in record time. Kayla answers her door in low-slung sweatpants and a tight, white tank top. The sight of her will never not take my breath away.

"What are you doing here?"

She might want to act like she wasn't expecting me, but I know it's all for show. Freshly showered and buzzing with nervous energy, I can tell she's been waiting. I've always loved her best in comfy clothes, and she knows it. The damp ends of her hair leave a wet spot near her nipples, and I can see the outline of them poking through the ribbed fabric. It's an effort to look at her face instead of them.

"Forgot to give you your Christmas present," I tell her, stepping inside and closing the door behind me.

"Is it your penis?" she asks, biting the side of her thumb. Her directness is one of the hottest things about her. Kayla tells it like it is and has no reservations about asking for what she wants.

"Is that what you asked Santa for?" I tease, scooping her damp hair behind her shoulders and bending to kiss the spot where it meets her neck. "You're very naughty."

"Shut up." She cups the front of my jeans where I'm already half-hard, grabs the back of my neck and pulls my mouth to hers. Kayla always smells incredible, but tonight she's somehow clean and sinful all at once. She opens first, her tongue running along my lower lip until I'm kissing her back, hard and hungry.

We've danced this dance a hundred times, her arms around my neck, my hands gripping her ass, lifting her to hook her legs around my waist. I should take my boots off, but getting inside her is my only priority right now.

In her room, I sit us both down at the end of her bed and tug her top straight off. Mine goes next, and then we're lost in a blur of hands and tongues, fighting to taste as much of each other as we can.

Kayla rolls her hips and grinds hard against my erection, painful at the thought of being inside her if we could only slow down for a second and focus on getting the right parts in the right place. I can't concentrate on shit when she's sucking at my neck and taking my earlobe between her teeth.

When I reach into my pocket for a condom, she hops off and removes my boots and the rest of our clothes. Before she has a chance to climb on top of me, I scoot further up the bed, half sitting against her pile of pillows.

Kayla is a vision, crawling up the bed towards me, eyes locked on mine. My cock twitches between us, anticipation flooding my system.

"Someone's eager," she giggles, and she's not wrong. Sex with Kayla is never predictable, and always incredible. We established early on we're both curious about a lot of things, and we love making each other happy. It's the perfect blend of give and take, and nobody is ever left disappointed.

"He's missed you."

"I saw him three days ago," she says, running one fingertip along the underside of my shaft.

"Not like this. I was too quick with you that night. He wants more."

"Oh yeah? Better make sure he's well looked after then."

Kneeling between my legs, she splays her hands over the top of my thighs, bends at the waist, and wraps her lips around the swollen tip. My head sinks deeper into the pillows, moans filling the room. My instinct is to cover my mouth, and I get a cheap thrill knowing neither of us will have to hold back tonight.

In the dim light of her bedroom, I watch her work me over with her tongue, long sweeping licks up one side of my shaft, then the other. She takes her time, watching me watch her while I fist the sheets at my hips.

"Get it messy," I tell her, and she takes it deeper, gagging on it before she pulls back and spits on it. She wraps both hands around me, stroking up the length and twisting back down. Nobody jerks me off like Kayla does, and though I've tried a thousand times, I can never do it as well as she does.

Perfect pressure, perfect pace, perfect woman.

"What's on your list this year?" she asks.

"Only you."

"You said it was miles long."

"Well..." I stifle a moan, hips tipping up while she pushes down. "Right now, I can't think of anything better than this."

She smiles, rubbing the head of my dick over her pretty lips. "I can."

"Oh, yeah?"

"You inside me. Bare." Her tongue swirls around me and I see stars. After all the things we've done together, she always finds something to make it even hotter.

"I've never... with anyone else... I've never."

"I haven't either, but I want to, if you do?"

My answer is a strangled moan when she sinks me deep into the back of her throat, twisting her way back up and releasing me with a wet pop.

"And I'm still on birth control, if that's what you're worried about."

"Come here," I beg, and she shifts to straddle me, her bare pussy hovering a few inches above my aching cock. I cup her face and smooth my thumbs across her cheeks, trying to get a read on her mood.

This is not something you should decide in the heat of the moment. If we're going to do this, I need her to know it means something to me.

"What I'm worried about is losing my cool and coming after five seconds inside you. I want to make it worth your time. Can I make you come first?"

Reaching between her legs, I find her swollen and ready, slick folds taking my fingers easily.

"I don't want to wait," she says, inching lower to rub herself where I'm rock hard and ready. "I don't care if we rush. It's always so good with you."

"Then take whatever you want, Bunny. I'm all yours."

My gaze focuses in on where she lines me up with her entrance, and we both gasp and jerk when the first inch slips inside. The sensation is like nothing else I've ever felt with her and I need a moment to get my shit under control, but Kayla grips my shoulders and works herself up and down the length.

My hands cup her hips as she rides me, watching my cock disappear between her thighs. Kayla was right. It's always so good between us, but there are no words for how incredible it is this time. I grip the back of her head and pull her down to kiss me, needing her close.

She switches her movements, groaning as she sinks right down, grinding her clit against me.

"Gonna come," she whispers into my mouth. "Fill me up. Please?"

Her pleading is all it takes to get me over the edge. Anything this woman ever asked me for, I'd bend over backwards to give her.

My arms wrap tight around her waist, pulling her down while my cock explodes, filling the space between us. I suck at her throat and her pussy clenches around me, thighs trembling by my hips, nails clutching at my skin.

Reaching between us, my thumb finds her clit, adding just enough pressure to get her there too. We cling to each other, hearts racing as pleasure floods her system and robs her of her words.

"Ryan?" she pants, her open mouth on my throat sending shivers down my spine. "Don't want to stop. Can you keep going?"

I've never come twice in a row, but if it could happen with anyone, it's going to be her.

Chapter 14
Kayla

Ryan flips me onto my back, and his mouth never leaves mine. His kisses are soft and tender, his hips rocking slowly in and out of me. Most of the times we've been together have been rushed, sneaky fucks before anyone notices we've slipped away. An entire night to take our time with each other is the best Christmas gift I could ever have asked for.

"Lift your knees up," he says, kneeling to watch where he leaks out of me. He drags the head of his cock through my aching flesh, scooping the warm fluid up to press back inside me, marking me in the deepest way. My spine presses into the mattress, and I hug my knees to my chest. The angle feels so good, so filthy and exposed.

My eyes close, lost in the sensation of him dragging his cock out right to the tip before plunging back in. The sound of him fucking his cum in and out of me is obscene, and I know I've been reading too many books with breeding kinks, because it's turning me on way more than it should.

He slips his hand between us, spreading it around as it spills out. I stick my tongue out and he lets me lick his fingers clean, trailing them down my throat, then rolling my nipple between them. When he splays his hand between my breasts, I know he's hunting for my heartbeat, and I reach out to touch him in the same way.

'Two hearts, one sky.'

Some soppy words we once said that clearly buried their way underneath our skin. I've never told him how I lay in bed at night, my hand in the same spot, wondering if he ever does it too.

His mouth opens and closes, and I pull him down to kiss me before he has the chance to say something that will ruin this moment. His pace slows, though the angle hits just right, and I wonder if there's a world where this is all we do. Him in my bed, mine to touch freely, safe in the knowledge we're not on some countdown to goodbye.

If not, could we somehow stop time, so I never have to look at anything but him. Those grey-green eyes, deep and full of everything I long to hear. They'd never close, never look away, and definitely never say *'see you next winter'* when he walks out of my life.

Tell me. Tell me. Tell me.

My heart begs to know what he's thinking, but I won't dare ask. I clench around him and his breath turns shaky, snapping us both out of our trance. He picks up his pace again, delicious, slow thrusts that make me feel like I'm floating. It's heaven, but I need more.

"Need you closer," I beg him, spreading my knees to make room for him to position himself between them.

"Don't want to crush you," he says, sucking my lip between his teeth.

"I want you to." I drag my nails down his back, dig them into his firm ass, and I pull him harder inside me. My hand finds my clit, slippery and swollen, and a few circles are all it takes to push me to the brink. I throw my head back against the pillow, my breasts pushing up against his warm chest.

"Yes, yes, yes," he whispers, staring into my soul, stroking back my hair as I shatter around his cock. My body convulses, and he holds me tight, hips bucking into me when he follows me over the edge a second time.

Other men roll over or fuck right off, but Ryan stays, both in the bed, and in the moment. I don't want to move, and there's no pressure to. Instead, he hums against my throat, strokes from the top of my shoulder all the way to my ankle and back again, as if to make sure he's touched every part of me.

While I come down and catch my breath, he fills my head with adoring whispers of *'so pretty'* and *'my girl'* and *'Kayla, oh, Kayla'*.

Getting over Ryan Richmond?

I never stood a fucking chance.

Chapter 15

Kayla

Seven Winters Ago / Age Twenty-One

The minute I dump my bags in my bedroom, I head straight back out and race up the hill to Ryan's house. He answers the door in checked pyjama pants and a hoodie, his hair sticking up all over the place.

After last year, I don't know how I expected him to react to seeing me. I still hate myself for wasting so much time I could have spent with him.

He leans against the doorframe with his arms folded across his chest. "How's the boyfriend?"

"There is no boyfriend," I tell him. "Do you have a girlfriend?"

He shakes his head and then I'm back in his arms with his lips on mine. Right where I'm supposed to be.

Chapter 16
Kayla

After a quick shower, I find Ryan stretched out face down on my bed, half asleep and so hot it hurts to look at him. His back glistens with a thin sheen of sweat, and I run one fingertip along the length of his spine, squeezing his perfect bum to rouse him from his slumber. He murmurs softly, twisting to face me. His hair is a mess from my fingers, his lips a little puffy from kissing so hard.

While I pull on fresh underwear and a t-shirt, my eye catches on something on the back of his arm and I panic. Did I grip him too tight while he fucked me? On closer inspection, it's too dark to be a bruise. Too intricate. When the lines fall into place, my hand flies to my mouth.

"What the hell is this?"

"Hmm?"

I climb on top of him, straddling his naked frame, and twist his bicep to get a better look.

"This."

A smile spreads across his face. "Oh that. I was wondering when you'd notice."

"Since when did you get a tattoo?"

"Since the first winter I didn't come home," he confesses, chipping off another piece of my heart.

My blood races as I slowly trace the outline with the tip of my nail. "Two skis."

"One for you, and one for me."

They're propped up in snow, the vast landscape looming behind. "And the mountain?"

"My favourite place in the world. Here with you."

He rolls over between my legs, and even though it's obvious I'm crying, I cover my eyes. "Fuck off, Ryan. You did not do that for me."

"I think I very clearly did, actually." His warm hands stroke the tops of my thighs, thumbs digging into the flesh at the top.

"Why are you like this?"

He sits up against the headboard and pulls me into my lap. I fit perfectly here, like it's where I belong. In those first few years after taking our friendship to the next level, all I wanted was for us to have this easy intimacy.

While my university friends were dating boys who they could kiss at parties and spend entire weekends with, I was dreaming of Ryan Richmond, the boy from the mountains who somehow knew me better than anyone.

Nothing about us makes sense. Sure, we have some things in common; our love of skiing and eating, our taste in music and films, our stubborn determination to beat each other at whatever challenge we throw down. Not to mention our insane levels of compatibility in the bedroom. Hell, half the shit I'm into is all because we've experimented together.

And that's pretty much it. It's not fair for two people to have this much chemistry, this much history, and no future. I've tangled and untangled the knot of us over and over. I've told myself we're nothing but two idiots who like to fuck and happen to be in the same location once a year.

Other times I've slipped hard in the opposite direction. Flirted with the fantasy of a life with him. Breakfasts, and weekends. Picking out bedsheets and paint swatches. Wedding dresses and babies.

That's how far gone I am for this man.

Two weeks a year doesn't mean you know a person, no matter how much of that time is spent in bed, at your most naked and vulnerable.

Some years, I've wanted to know everything. What does his bedroom look like? Who are his friends? What does he look like on the beaches of California?

Aged nine, I asked my parents for his address, convinced we could become pen-pals, but they didn't know it, and our grandparents had passed away, so I couldn't ask them either. The following winter, it seemed daft to have even considered writing to each other. The joy of winter with Ryan was all in the build-up, in catching up and telling stories. It wouldn't have been so fun if I'd heard them all before.

Now, it's easier to pretend I don't care if I don't ask about his life. L.A., other women, his job. Who gives a shit about all that?

I do. Unfortunately.

I care so much it hurts, even when he's here, and all mine. There's a pinch behind my ribs, my little heart warning me. It knows it's heading for war, and I know there's no way to avoid it.

Ryan pulls my hands away from my face and presses kisses to each fingertip.

"What's wrong?"

"We don't talk all this time and you're off getting secret tattoos for me?"

He tucks loose strands of my hair behind my ears, thumb sweeping away a tear that's spilled over. "I got it for me, mostly."

"Why?"

"I didn't have anything of yours, and I wanted to always keep a part of you with me."

The rest of my heart shatters, and I know there's no way I can put it back together on my own.

"You cannot be serious." I wrap my hand around the base of his throat and pretend to throttle him.

"Is that a problem?"

"Yes, it's a problem, Ryan. I'm trying really fucking hard to get over you and you're making it impossible."

"Why are you trying to get over me?"

When he asked at the parade if he could see me today, I should have said no. I knew if I let my guard down, I'd undo all the work I've done to get over him. He could have taken his sexy ass and his secret tattoo back to California, and I could have lived a perfectly reasonable life without ever knowing anything about it.

Now he's here, all naked and golden, and I know I'd never have said no. His lopsided smile belongs to both the boy I fell for first, and the man I'll never get over. He's part of all of my best memories, and now we're deep under each other's skin.

Accepting we have no future has been a work in progress. Tattoos make us a permanent part of each other, and I'm too tired, too emotionally wrung out, to think about what any of this means for us.

Fuck it. He'll find out, eventually.

I twist in his lap until he can see the back of my arm, and he gasps.

"Two skis," he says, tugging my elbow back so he can press his mouth to the spot that bears similar markings. He doesn't kiss it, just holds his lips there in some sort of silent worship.

"One for you and one for me," I whisper.

Repeating his words is no lie, even though I've never confessed the true meaning of my tattoo to anyone else. My design is more simple than his, two line drawings crossed in the shape of an X. You can't even tell they are skis unless you're up close, and so few people are.

"When?" he whispers, and the lump in my throat doubles in size.

"Around the same time, I guess."

It was a spontaneous decision. I was meeting a friend for lunch and walked past a tattoo shop in Edinburgh. Even now I couldn't tell you what called me to go inside, but before I knew it, I was in the chair and marked forever.

To think he was doing the same on the other side of the world has me believing in invisible strings and soulmates and forevers. The very stuff I've trained myself to ignore. *'Soulmates'* is a dangerous concept to entertain when there are thousands of miles keeping you apart.

"Baby." His breath shudders out against my skin, and I twist back to hold him close against my chest. His arms tighten around me, and he buries his face in the crook of my neck, a spot he once told me was his happy place.

'Baby' is new.

Soft.

More.

He whispers it again, right into the skin of my throat.

"I'm so sorry I didn't come back. I don't know what the fuck I was thinking."

This wasn't supposed to happen. I was going to let myself enjoy his company for one last year and move on. There's no way I can tell him to leave now.

His fingertips trace patterns up my spine, remind me of a night we spent hours pretending to write words on each others backs and guessing what they were. I thought about writing *'I love you'* but hoped he'd do it first.

"You're so fucking beautiful. I thought about you every day, you know that?"

As scary as it is, I believe him, because I thought of him every day, too. They weren't always good thoughts. Sometimes I wished for his dick to fall off, or worse, for his dream career to fail, so he wouldn't have anything to keep him from me. Cold, selfish thoughts mixed in with a million dirty ones. I'm not sure I've ever had an orgasm without picturing him behind my eyelids.

Ryan flips me onto my back and pulls the covers up and over our heads.

"Let me make it up to you," he says, kissing a soft trail down past my belly. "Ask me for what you want."

I want you to stay.

The thought is more fucked up than anything physical I could ever ask for. With sex, I know he'd give me anything I desired, and I hate my brain for thinking of things he'll never be able to offer.

"Ask me," he growls, taking a chunk of thigh between his teeth.

Sinking my fingers through the strands of his hair, I hitch one knee up to the side and make room for him to taste me.

"Just this. Just you. Just like that."

Chapter 17

Ryan

Eight Winters Ago / Age Twenty

Kayla's parents are hosting my family for our first night back in the mountains and they've fixed an incredible spread of local delicacies.

My parents told me she's been lodging with a local family this winter while she does her instructor training. Turning her love of skiing into a job has always been a dream of Kayla's, and I can't wait to hear about it when I finally get her to myself.

After dinner, she and I clear the table and when we find ourselves alone in the kitchen, I loop my arms around her waist, pull her close and bury my face in her neck.

"Woah, woah, woah," she says, twisting out of my hold and pressing her palms against my chest. "I have a boyfriend."

The laugh that rumbles out of me is involuntary, because this is so far from funny. I don't know how else to react. Kayla squares off with me, hands on her hips, head cocked to one side.

"It's not funny."

"Damn right it's not funny. Is it serious?"

It's the first in a series of questions that spring to mind, along with what the fuck? Since when? Who the fuck is he? Are you winding me up? And, once again, what the actual fuck?

There are a few women I've dated at college this year, and that's been a fun time, but I was careful not to let anything get serious or carry on too close to the holidays. I'm shocked Kayla wasn't considerate enough to do the same.

She lowers her voice and pokes her head around the kitchen door to make sure nobody is listening. "Serious enough, I'm not going to cheat on him, if sex is what you're after."

Er, yeah, that's what I'm after.

That's our whole fucking deal. I only spend three hundred and fifty-one days of the year looking forward to the fourteen when I'll get to touch her again. My wishlist has about fifty things on it, none of which included her and some other guy.

"Does he live here?"

"Yes, he's on the same course as me."

"Are you going to marry him?"

She scoffs, and starts stacking the dishwasher, her back to me. "I'm twenty, Ryan, give me a break."

"But what if you do?"

What if I never get to touch you again?

We still hang out a bit, still race each other all over the mountain, still catch chocolate coins from *Père Noël* at the parade, but everything is different now. So when a pretty Italian girl tries to kiss me at Rico's, I don't say no. And when she invites me back to her hotel, I don't say no to that either.

Chapter 18
Ryan

Kayla and I skied together on Boxing Day, but she's leading a tour today, and Hannah's taken Cameron out for more ski practice. I've chilled out at home all day.

We've barely had any time for the three of us to hang out and race each other like old times, but I guess that's my fault for bringing a beginner to the mountains.

It's probably a good thing he's here to keep my sister company. Once Kayla and I struck up our deal, we used to feel guilty about ditching Hannah. Until we had our hands down each other's ski-pants, that is.

I need the rest after our last two nights together, anyway. Nights where we stayed up for hours, talking and laughing until someone's hand landed on someone's thigh, or our mouths got too close and conversation turned to kissing without us even noticing.

Every day with Kayla is better than the last. Before this trip, one of us has always had to sneak out, so we've only slept over a couple of times. Getting to hold her all night, her ass pressed against me, my nose buried in the nape of her neck was fucking heaven.

So why do I feel like utter shit? Seeing her cry when she discovered my tattoo was awful, but finding out she has an almost identical one hurt even more.

Skipping Christmas two years ago wasn't an easy decision, but I thought it was for the best for both of us. Knowing she's struggled to move on too makes me see what a huge mistake that was.

I could have lost her, lost everything, but I don't know where we go from here. We can't be together, but we clearly don't want to be apart.

All Kayla has ever wanted is to live in the mountains. As soon as she was old enough, she was passing all kinds of instructor qualifications to build a life out here.

And ever since Dad took us along to the film sets of some of his more famous clients, all I've ever wanted is to work in the industry. Could I move here? It's unlikely. This is Hollywood, for fuck's sake, there's no other opportunity like it.

I work hard, I'm reliable, and good at what I do. I've made good connections in the industry, and I think my workload could stay steady for as long as I want it to. My French isn't good enough to make it over here. There are studios in London, but is that any better? It's not like we ever entertained the idea of doing a long distance thing when I lived in London and she lived in Edinburgh.

What's the point of being in a relationship if they aren't close by? I don't want to be with someone I can't hold at night, can't cook dinner for, can't curl up with on the sofa at the end of a long day. Still, if there was one thing worth giving all of this up for, it would be her.

After a dinner of leftovers, we hang out on the sofas, but our quiet contentment doesn't last long.

"For God's sake, Ryan," Mum says, fussing around with the curtains by the window that overlook the ski slopes.

"What did I do now?"

She points one angry finger at the ground. "Why is there a condom wrapper on the floor over here?"

"That's not mine!" I protest. Hannah and Cameron look mortified and when they both say *'it's mine'*, I put two and two together and see red.

While I've been trying to fix things with Kayla, my best friend has been fooling around with my sister? The man who tells the world about his sexual exploits for a living, and my little sister who's had her heart broken so badly she couldn't get out of bed for weeks?

My sister?

Absolutely fucking not.

I'm on my feet in a heartbeat, there's a scuffle and screaming, and the next thing I know, Dad is dragging us both out to the balcony.

"I'm not wearing shoes!" I yell at him, but he clicks the closed door behind him and leaves me and Cameron out in the cold. Cameron backs away one hand up in surrender, the other rubbing the spot where my fist connected with his ribs. Or was it my knee? Either way, both hurt.

"What the fuck are you playing at? How could you do this to me? To her?"

"I'm falling in love with her, and trust me, I know it's fucking crazy."

"Damn right it's crazy. How is this gonna work? You don't live anywhere near her and long distance is a fucking nightmare."

"We haven't really had that conversation yet, so I don't know. Maybe I'll move to London or something."

"You just met her! What about all the other women you fuck for your content?"

"Fuck's sake, man. That's not what my work is."

I know enough to know he's into all kinds of shit. The one time curiosity got the better of me, I found a post about fucking some woman in a club bathroom, and another about letting a woman use her toys on him.

Sometimes he gets approached by women when we go out, and he has fans all over the world who'd be willing to drop to their knees and suck his dick in a heartbeat.

How he can be that way with anyone he meets is beyond me. I have no trouble meeting women either, but when things go further, I get too in my head. All I can picture is her. I've only ever had that connection with Kayla, and it pisses me off Cam can fuck around with anyone, with zero consequences.

"My fucking sister!"

"We haven't done anything she hasn't been 100% OK with, Ryan. You know I'm not like that. What are you actually mad about? Is it Kayla?"

"Oh, fuck off."

The balcony floor is wet and freezing, and I hop from one foot to the other until Dad lets us back inside. Hannah looks upset, Mum looks furious, but I ignore them all and storm upstairs to my room.

Cameron asked me about her on the flight over, and I explicitly told him not to hit on her. Hannah doesn't fuck around like this. How did this even happen?

My head is still swimming when she comes to clear the air. It turns out she already knew about Cameron's alter-ego, and this whole thing has taken them by surprise too. She rips me a new one for acting like a dick and makes it clear I don't need to fight battles for her.

She might not be a teenager anymore, but that doesn't mean I don't have her best interests at heart. The thought of them together is stressing me out, but I trust her judgement, and if Hannah says she's OK, I have no choice but to believe her.

Plus, Cameron is my roommate and my ticket home. It's not like I can kick him out of here and never speak to him again.

Once I've had enough of sulking in my room, I find them all downstairs drinking Dad's special hot chocolate, clearly avoiding the subject of what just went down.

"You wanna go to Rico's?" I grunt in Cameron's general direction.

He finishes his drink and thanks my dad before getting up. "I'll grab the sledges."

Hannah offers me a grateful smile, but Cameron's not the only one I need to make it up to.

"You're coming too, sis."

Chapter 19
Ryan

WHILE MY SISTER GETS drinks at the bar, Cameron tries to smooth things over, telling me the same story Hannah told me at the house.

I'm in no mood to hear it, but I am surprised to learn she told him all about the exes who treated her like shit. She's had a hard time trusting anyone since they fucked her over, so that must count for something good.

We probably have a lot more to talk about before I can get cool with this, and I have no idea how it will play out long term, but it's a start. My sister means the world to me, but I don't want to lose his friendship either.

"Look who I found," Hannah says, returning with Kayla by her side. She's still in her ski gear after a day of lessons, but she looks gorgeous as ever.

Unlike the four tequila shots in her hands.

"Let's celebrate you two being out in the open, shall we?" she says, setting them on the table and hopping up onto the barstool next to me.

"You knew?"

"Er, yeah. Look at them," she says, waving her hand in their direction. "I knew the second I laid eyes on him they were hot for each other. God, Ryan, you're such a dumbass. How did you not notice?"

I grip the leg of her stool and drag it closer to mine. "I must have been too busy looking at you."

"I thought we were being subtle," Hannah says, burying her face in her hands.

"Please," Kayla laughs. "You were not subtle at all. I saw you kissing on the slopes while I was teaching the other day. And holding hands at the parade."

I wouldn't have noticed, I was too busy trying to hold *her* hand. Across the table, Cameron brings Hannah's hand to his mouth and holds it there. How can this be happening?

Hannah glares at me when I grunt at the sight of the two of them. "Stop it. We're both consenting adults. We don't need your permission to do what we want."

"I don't see this ending in anything but disaster. You live thousands of miles apart."

"Ryan, stop being such a little shit," Kayla says, smacking me on the arm a lot harder than I deserve. "Some people don't need to be together all the time. You should know that better than anyone."

What the fuck is that supposed to mean?

Cam points his finger at her, holding his shot glass up. "I like this girl. She's smart."

"To long distance lovers," she cheers and they all toss their drinks back.

A few rounds of drinks and cards later, and my head is fuzzy in a different way. The music's too loud, the bar is too crowded, and my emotions are getting the better of me. My leg starts twitching and Kayla squeezes my thigh to ground me.

"Are you coming back to mine?" she asks, booping me on the nose. There's nowhere else I'd rather be.

Chapter 20
Kayla

Outside Rico's, we say our goodbyes, and I hang back a little while Ryan fistbumps Cameron. It's the best they'll manage under current circumstances. Yes, I saw this coming a mile off, but I can understand why it would be a shock for Ryan.

Hannah told me how their secret was discovered, and I would simply never return home if that happened to me. Ryan and I have always been pretty careful with our sneaking around, though we're not faultless.

Four years ago, we got busted kissing on his sofa after we thought everyone was asleep. If his dad had waited thirty more seconds to get a glass of water, he'd have definitely seen me topless. Instead, he covered his eyes and walked straight past the two of us, who were frozen in place, leaving with a cheery *'I saw nothing'*.

Hannah and Cameron head off with their sledges in hand, ready to make the journey back down to the Richmond house. I loop my arm around Ryan's waist and lead him in the opposite direction.

"Are you ok?" I ask.

"Do I have a choice? It's my sister and my best friend, I can't exactly avoid them."

I hug him closer when a crowd spills out of another bar, making space for them to pass us on the narrow pavement. "You worry about her."

"I don't want her getting into a long distance thing. It won't work."

"Why wouldn't it work?"

"Because we don't," he grunts.

"Oh, come on, that's different and you know it. If they want to make it work, I'm sure they'll find a way."

I barely know Cameron, but I know Hannah. She doesn't take risks, was always the smart voice of reason when Ryan and I wanted to get up to mischief as kids. She wouldn't get into something with him if she hadn't weighed up all the pros and cons first.

Whenever I've considered the possibility of something more serious with Ryan, my entire list is cons.

He stops walking, and my arm slips loose from his waist. Beneath the glow of a streetlamp, his expression is so forlorn it makes my chest hurt. I want to look away, but I can't, not when I know he's being sincere.

"What if I want to make it work, Kayla?" His soft words suck all the air from my lungs.

For almost a decade, all I've wanted is this. Not a sign, not a feeling, but actual concrete words. Proof he wants me the way I want him. Now I have it, I wish he'd take it back. It's too late.

"I said, what if I want to make it work?"

My feet stay rooted to the spot, even when he reaches out to pull me back into his arms. I land with my palms against his chest. Normally, I can't get close enough, but this is suffocating.

"Why are you saying this now?"

His hands sweep from my shoulders down to my elbows and back up to my wrists. He circles them with his fingers, thumbs pressing into my pulse point as if he's checking I'm real. There's some muscle memory there, but I can't place it while my head is full of his words.

"I missed you so much, and I know I should have tried to get in touch with you. That was a dumb fucking move on my part, but I can't imagine going home and waving you off with a *'see you next winter'* anymore. That's not going to be enough for me."

"We couldn't make it work when I was in Edinburgh and you were in London. What on earth makes you think we can make it work between here and L.A.? The time difference would kill us if the distance didn't."

Me. It would kill me.

"We've never really tried! It's only nine hours. I'll call you before I go to bed and we can chat while you eat your breakfast. Then I'll call you before I start work and you'll be getting home."

"That's ridiculous," I say, tugging my hands back. "Do you hear yourself? I don't want a relationship based on phone calls."

"But you *do* want a relationship with me?"

"That's not what I said."

"Please, Kayla? Please give us a chance."

"It's not what I want, Ryan!" I yell.

"You don't want me?"

"Stop twisting my words." A woman across the street stops to assess the situation. I wave her on and lower my voice. "You're not being fair. You can't abandon me for three years and expect me to agree to a long distance relationship just because your sister and your friend have hooked up and you're feeling some kind of way about it. There's no world where you and I work."

His face crumples, and he looks up at the stars, but it's too late. I've already seen the exact moment I break his heart.

"Ryan, don't cry."

"I'm not crying."

Even in the dim light, there's no hiding his tears. I cup his cheeks, tilt his head back down to mine, and brush them away with my thumb. There's nothing worse than seeing him hurting. I'd take all the pain and bear it myself if it meant I could get his smile back.

"This fucking sucks. And it hurts so much," he shudders out, and I nod and sniff back my own tears. "Can we go home?"

"To mine?" I wouldn't blame him if he'd changed his mind. About tonight, and about me. He nods, wiping his eyes with the back of his hand, and we carry on in silence.

In my apartment, I help him out of his jacket and shoes. He's not even drunk, just emotional and exhausted, which is no surprise given how little sleep we've had these past few nights. Between sex and skiing, my thighs have never worked so hard.

He lets me take his hand and lead him to the living room. I flick on a side lamp, sit him down on the sofa, and rush to change out of my ski gear and into comfy clothes. I half expect to find him asleep, but when I sit down, he shifts to rest his head in my lap.

We were teenagers, half-watching some dumb Christmas movie the first time we did this. A play fight that started with innocent tickling and ended up with us panting for breath and him looking up at me the way he is now. Our first kiss happened the very next day. I always thought that was the point of no return for us, but I think we were entwined long before then.

Smoothing his hair back off his face, he hums contentedly, leaning into my touch. It's a dangerous cycle. Even in pain, we find comfort in each other, only for that comfort to turn into more pain when we go our separate ways.

The only thing worse than having him for only two weeks of the year, would be knowing he's mine, but getting none of the benefits. None of the closeness, the kisses, the knowing smiles across a room.

We'd have to go about our separate lives never getting a goodnight hug or grabbing lunch together. We aren't cut out for that kind of torture.

"I thought I could get over you," he says quietly. "But I couldn't, and I hated you telling me you tried to get over me, too."

"Shh, it's late. We don't have to talk about it."

"You said you couldn't think of anything worse than loving me."

"What?"

"The last time I saw you. That's what you said." His arm snakes around my back, and presses his cheek against my belly, the weight of it all rushing out in a sigh. "You said it and I snuck out the next morning and I felt so bad I puked in a bin at the airport."

"Oh, God."

The hot tub, my almost-confession.

I press the heels of my palms into my eye sockets until it hurts. That wasn't what I meant, and anyway, it was ridiculous to pretend I couldn't love him when I already did. And still do.

I've interrogated the memory of that last night countless times, picking it apart to figure out where we went wrong. Tangled in sheets, he'd slipped out while I was in such a state of bliss I hadn't fully registered *'see you next winter'* passed my lips. Was he mad I didn't say a proper goodbye? Should I have been mad he didn't either?

"It was never because I didn't want you," he continues. "It's because I wanted you so much it scared me you might not want me back. I thought it was for the best, throwing myself into work and trying not to think about you."

"That's why you didn't come back?"

He nods and sniffs. "The first year, I really did have to work. Production was behind, I pulled eighteen-hour days to keep things on track. It was the worst Christmas ever."

"And last year?"

"Honestly? There's no reason I couldn't have come last year."

"The redhead. Was she the reason you stayed?"

He twists his head and takes a deep, shaky breath.

"I told you we were never serious. I was coming, I had a ticket booked, and I'd have called it off with her, but I got in my head and convinced myself you'd probably met someone."

That is the exact reason why this is impossible, and why our pact needs to end. It isn't sustainable. One of these days we'll meet other people who we want something more from, and if that happened while we'd made some sort of commitment to each other, we'd never recover. I certainly wouldn't be able to live here, surrounded by memories of him.

How long can we keep doing this? Am I going to die knowing I had a lot of great sex but nobody ever truly loved me because I held out for him?

"Well, what if I had Ryan? What if I was seeing someone this year?"

"I'd have kicked his ass," he grumbles, throwing me his best frown.

"Same way you kicked Cameron's ass earlier and got turfed out in the cold by your dad?" His eyebrows knit together, and I smooth them out with my thumb. "Hannah told me."

"I shouldn't have done that," he says.

"You've been drinking. Let's forget this conversation happened and go get some sleep."

"I can't forget anything about you. Not ever. You're my North Star. You always guide me home."

He pulls a blanket from the back of the sofa and drapes it over us. We lay entwined for a while, in silence but for the sound of our breathing and the low hum of the refrigerator. Outside, the moon is full and high above the mountain. When we were kids, it gave me such comfort to know we could look up and see the same sky, same stars. We never get the chance now we live in different time zones.

"Can you lie to me?" he asks sleepily.

"Hmm?"

"I know you said there's no world where we work, but can you pretend, like old times?"

"Ryan." My eyes squeeze shut, and he rolls to his side, burrowing his face against my stomach.

"Please?"

We should be happy right now. He's here, in my arms, and in my house. It should be enough, but it's torture, and the more we do this, the worse it gets. A little daydreaming can't make it any more painful than it already is.

"Somewhere…" I whisper, stroking his hair in smooth, slow motions. "Somewhere, there's a world where we're together. You wake up in my arms every morning, you feel my heart beating against your cheek. Some days you make the coffee, some days it's my turn, but you always come back and drink it in bed. I scrub your back in the shower, and you wash my hair. We ski every day, eat pizza for lunch. You're mine, and I'm yours, and we are so, so happy."

Long after he's fallen asleep, I keep going, spilling my heart out, wiping my tears before they can drip onto his face. I tell him everything, all those worlds I've pictured, every wish I've ever made, even though I know they don't stand a hope in hell of coming true.

Chapter 21

Ryan

Nine Winters Ago / Age Nineteen

While Kayla gets dressed, I tie off the condom, wrap it in tissue and bury it deep in her wastepaper basket. We told our parents we were going to ski in the next valley, but bunking off and heading back to her empty house was a much better idea.

In the mirror, she tugs her braids loose and brushes the knots out of her hair from where I've messed it up at the back.

"I like doing this with you," she says. "The sex stuff."

"Yeah?" *Thank fuck for that.* "Me too."

"Do you think we can try reverse cowgirl next time?"

Standing behind her, I kiss my way up the side of her neck, my hand sneaking underneath her loose t-shirt. "Um, yes, definitely. That sounds hot."

"Have you done it before?" she asks, then shakes her head. "Sorry, I know I'm not supposed to ask."

"It's OK. No, I haven't done it before."

I haven't done it before because she's still the only person I've slept with, but I don't know if she'd think that was a good or bad thing. I don't want her to think I'm a loser who can't get laid, but the couple of times I've had the opportunity, the only person I wanted was her.

She spins to face me, twisting her hair into a bun and fixing it in place on the top of her head. "Is there anything you want to try?"

"What do you mean?"

"Any stuff you're curious about? Don't you think it makes sense for us to use each other? For practice?"

"Is that what this is? Us using each other?"

"Don't make it sound like a bad thing. I like knowing I can come here and try stuff with you. You're a safe bet. We're clearly hot for each other, but there's no way we can get attached and make a mess of this."

There's a twisting feeling in the pit of my stomach. Turning other girls down because I'd rather be with her kind of feels like I might already be attached here.

"What kind of stuff are we talking about here?"

"I don't know," she shrugs. "Positions, places. Whatever you want."

"Well, what's on your wishlist?"

"Shower sex, hot tub. Oh, and I want to try sucking your dick with my head hanging over the edge of the bed," she adds casually, like we're talking about grocery lists and not getting each other off. "I hear you can get it deeper that way."

"Wow, you've really put a lot of thought into this."

"Well, I've had an entire year to think about it." I wonder if that means she hasn't been hooking up with other people, but I don't ask.

Chapter 22
Kayla

We're supposed to be getting ready for dinner with our parents and Hannah and Cameron, so obviously we're naked in my bed. Ryan is sprawled out sideways, sweaty and spent, with his head in my lap. My fingers are doing a terrible job of smoothing his hair back down from where I've mussed it up, but Ryan's hair has always been inclined to do what it wants.

Trapped in this liminal, post-orgasmic haze, we don't talk, just lay there watching each other, hands creeping wherever they please. It's already dark outside. Why would we get up? If we stay here, I won't have to think about the end of the trip, or the end of us.

There was a time when I loved the annual New Year's Eve fireworks display. We got to stay up extra late, strangers always gave us even more chocolate, and our grandmothers taught us to make wishes on the first explosion.

In recent years, the end of December is not much more than a crappy reminder we only have a few days left together. No amount of fireworks or chocolates could convince me there's a better plan than staying in bed.

"I think we should keep talking. When I go home," he says, spoiling the mood. My body tenses underneath him, and he reaches up to splay his hand across my heart. "You don't agree?"

We haven't talked about our conversation the other night, but my thoughts haven't stopped going round and round in circles. In the hundreds, if not thousands, of hours I've spent thinking of him when we've been apart, I've run every possible scenario.

He moves closer to me, or I move closer to him, or we both move somewhere else entirely. Every option leads to the same conclusion: one or both of us would be miserable. Sticking it out as friends is the least miserable option.

Being together and not being able to see him, touch him, fuck him, would absolutely suck. I'm not the sort of person who could do long distance. The mere thought of it makes me feel ill.

"I think it would be too painful," I tell him quietly.

His eyebrows knit together, and his hand slides up to flex his fingers over my heart. "I won't hurt you."

"I know you won't, but it already hurts, and we're not a couple. So no, I don't think it would be a good idea to keep talking."

"Not even as friends? I don't want to live a life where you're not in it anymore."

"You're only saying that because your hand is on my boob."

His thumb rolls over my nipple while his other hand strokes up the inside of my thigh. It's tempting to let him keep going, but this conversation has me feeling unsettled.

The more he pushes me on the subject of us, the more I want to push him away. And that's not really what I want at all, I don't see a way through. He shifts to hover over me, but I roll out from underneath his arms and head for the bathroom.

"Where are you going?" he whines, like he didn't already get to come in my mouth fifteen minutes ago.

"We should get dressed. I'm not explaining this when my mum calls to ask why neither of us are at dinner."

Later, we stomp halfway up the pitch black slope behind our houses, to the special spot we always watch the fireworks from. Ryan and I sit back from our families, cold bottoms in the snow, our hands linked behind our backs.

Everyone knows, but nobody ever acknowledges us. They probably don't know how to label it, and why would they? We make enough of a mess of it ourselves.

The display is as glorious as ever. Bright golds and shimmering silvers lighting up the sky above the valley. A chorus of *oohs* and *ahhs* come in all directions, and when I sneak glances in Ryan's direction, his smile is wide and boyish. I rest my head on his shoulder and he wraps his arm around my back. Who cares if we have an audience?

"What did you wish for?" he asks when it's all over.

"Same thing I wish for every year."

"And it still hasn't come true? You must have been a very naughty girl indeed."

"Wishes aren't like Santa, Ryan. It's not something you can ask for. It's something you hope will come true."

"Fair enough," he teases. "You were pretty naughty riding my face earlier, though."

"*Shhh!*" I hiss, balling up a sneaky handful of snow in my other fist. "You shush."

Further down the hill, Hannah crouches beside Cameron, pretending to tie her shoelace. My lips pinch together and I hold Ryan close.

I've never known if the men simply forget, or if they let us have the win, but I wait for my mum's signal and then it's war. My fist flies up, fresh powder shoved deep into the collar of Ryan's jacket. Mum's snowball goes down the back of Dad's trousers, and Cameron's shriek is louder than anyone's. It almost stops me in my tracks, but I'm up and bolting for the treeline before Ryan can get his revenge.

He's quick, grabbing the tail end of my scarf to pull me backwards. I slip it over my head and keep going, leaving our families to battle it out behind us. I'm barely into the woods when I trip, and I squeeze my eyes shut, certain I'm about to eat dirt. When I open them, I'm hovering inches from the ground, the back of my jacket caught in Ryan's fist.

He hauls me up and marches me over to a nearby trunk, spinning me to face him. His other hand is full of snow, primed and ready to attack.

"You're getting spanked for that later."

Heat floods south, and I dart my tongue out to lick his lips. "So you keep threatening, but I don't see any handprints."

He growls, and I remember how much a little bratty attitude turns him on. As if I could forget. If I'm going to pay for it, I'll gladly be on my worst behaviour.

"Tell me what you wished for," he says, holding the snow closer.

"Never!"

"Well, whatever it is, I hope you get it."

Not once have I asked him what he wishes for. Partly because I always believed my grandma's warning that if you tell someone your wish, then it won't come true. Mostly out of fear he wishes for something that has nothing to do with me.

I take the deepest breath I can before he smashes his snowball in my face, then I get my own back by gripping the front of his jacket and burying my frozen cheek against his neck. It's the perfect mix of hot and cold, the scent of fresh snow mixing with the scent of his skin.

Then his tongue is in my mouth, my head tipped back against the tree trunk, his knee between my thighs.

If we never have another winter together, at least we had this.

Chapter 23
Kayla

January third comes too fast. In a heartbeat, we're out of time.

Our parents are staying until tomorrow, but Hannah is on the same flight to London as Ryan and Cameron, who have a short layover before they head home to L.A.

Thankfully, it's changeover day in the resort, and I have no clients as one set leaves before the next group arrives. Desperate to eke out every moment I can spend with him, I offer to drive them all to the airport.

All the way down the mountain, I curse the winding roads for making me keep both hands on the wheel when I wish I could hold one of his instead.

The smart move would be to drop them outside, wave goodbye, and cry all the way back up the mountain, but I'm in too deep. I take the hit on airport parking so I can head into the terminal with them, and Ryan holds my hand the entire time.

Hannah and Cameron can't stop touching each other either as they walk ahead of us, but nobody seems to be staving off an internal breakdown the way I am. I can't even look at him.

We've barely spoken all morning, only communicating through longing stares and half-hearted smiles. Mark made me one of his special hot chocolates and I drank it downstairs while Ryan packed. Not much was said then either.

Everything feels different this time, and I can't imagine how much harder it would be if we were actually committing to something serious.

We'd left with plenty of time so they wouldn't have to rush through security, but now I wish for the opposite. I wish there was some urgency. His flight boarding, the gate calling, last call for passenger Ryan Richmond. Any other reason for him to go, something beyond our control.

"This wasn't long enough," Ryan says, pulling me close and pressing a kiss to my temple.

He needs to stop. I'm not strong enough for this goodbye, and I won't survive if he keeps talking. I bury my face in his chest so he won't see my tears, and he cups the back of my head.

"It's never long enough."

He holds my hand to his heart as mine pounds out a plea.

Stay. Stay. Stay.

Of course he won't stay. How could he possibly? There's no world in which I get what I want here.

"Hey Ryan?" I whisper against his chest.

Asking changes everything. I definitely won't ask.

"Yeah, baby?"

"Can I have your phone number?"

Shit.

He pulls back, cupping my face to tip it up to his. "You want to keep talking?"

"If you do?" There's a half-second where I swear my heart stops, so convinced he's going to say no, I scramble to argue my case. "We'll still be just friends, obviously. We can keep to the same arrangement as always, but with, I don't know, the occasional hello."

"How occasional?" The tip of his nose strokes up and down the length of mine.

"I don't need you to call me every day," I tell him, though I already know I'll be tempted to.

"What if I'm a menace and I text you all the time?"

"Do you want my number or not, asshole?"

He kisses one corner of my mouth, then the other. "Best friend I ever had."

He delves into his jacket pocket, unlocks his phone and hands it over. With bleary eyes, I'm not even sure I know what numbers are right now.

"You'd better call me in case I typed it wrong."

My phone buzzes in my pocket and I try not to laugh while I add Ryan Richmond to my contacts for the first time. This is a thing you do with strangers, not a man you've known your whole life, who's seen you in your best and worst moments, your most naked and vulnerable.

He pulls me in close again, opening the front of his jacket so I can slip my hands inside and around his back.

"I miss you already," I tell him. I'm so close to confessing what I wished for on the first firework, but it won't make a difference.

"Kayla," he whispers against my hair. "It's you in every world. You know that, right?"

Every world except this one.

When we finally let go, Hannah is waiting to give me a hug goodbye, with tears in her eyes, too. Part of me feels sad we didn't get to hang out much this winter. Ryan and I were always closer, but she's been a good friend, especially in those years he didn't come home.

"I feel like I've barely seen you this trip," I sob, and she chuckles softly against my shoulder.

"I was kind of pre-occupied."

Knowing she's willingly getting herself into a similar long-distance situation makes me feel a kind of twisted bond with her, even though she's much happier about it than I am.

"Are you OK?" she asks.

"What the fuck is wrong with us, Han?" I laugh, wiping my eyes behind her back. Mascara was a mistake, I must look ridiculous. "They're just boys."

"Boys we love," she offers, as if that excuses crying in the airport.

"We've never said that to each other," I whisper into her hair, and she squeezes me tighter.

"Doesn't mean it isn't true."

Any time I've come even close to entertaining thoughts of love, I've shoved them deep, deep down. That's not for us. Who in their right mind would let themselves fall in love with someone who lives so far away?

Now I live here permanently, it's worse than ever. It's so much easier to be the one who leaves. Ryan gets to fly home, go back to work, his friends, his life. Being the one who goes back to an empty apartment is a unique hell.

How am I supposed to sleep in my bed tonight, on a pillow that still smells like him, knowing it will be months until he comes back? How am I supposed to go about my daily life feeling like a part of me is missing? No amount of hiking or beer or cheese will fill the void.

"Right, this is embarrassing now," I say, letting her go and wiping my eyes. "You need to go live it up in the lounge or whatever it is you fancy business class folks do."

Ryan spins me back into his arms. "I'll see you next winter, but I'll talk to you sooner. OK, Bunny?"

"See you next winter," I nod, tears spilling faster than he can wipe them away. "You've got to go."

Waving them off through the first checkpoint, I dig my car keys into my palm, desperate to feel something worse than this pain. Except I was right, there is nothing worse than the pain of being miles away from the man you love.

When they disappear around the corner, it takes everything in me not to drop to the floor and bawl my eyes out. My phone buzzes in my pocket, pulling my focus for long enough to keep me vertical.

> **RYAN:** Miss you already

God, I hope I don't regret this. On the drive back up the mountain, it occurs to me nobody *'lets themselves'* fall in love. Love comes for you whether or not you want it to.

As predicted, I cry the entire way home, and even harder when I find the t-shirt he's left under my pillow.

Chapter 24

Ryan

RYAN: Good Morning Bunny

KAYLA: Shouldn't you be sleeping?

RYAN: About to head to bed. Longest day ever. Got time to talk?

KAYLA: Sorry, already on the ski lift. Try you later?

RYAN: Sure, have a great day!

TWO MISSED CALLS: KAYLA

> **RYAN:** Sorry had to work through lunch today. I'll try you later?

> **KAYLA:** I'm at dinner with clients tonight. Catch you in the morning?

> **KAYLA:** My morning, your bedtime

ONE MISSED CALL: KAYLA

> **RYAN:** Sorry I missed you, was wiped after a long day in the studio

> **RYAN:** Send me a pic, I miss your face, friend

Chapter 25
Kayla

March is the busiest month in the season, with perfect snow conditions, and families from all over the world descending on the resort for their winter vacations. I have tours or lessons booked every single day, sometimes multiple, and by the time I crash into bed at night, Ryan is busy at work.

Our schedules don't match up often enough to talk on the phone regularly, but we sustain our friendship with text messages, the occasional photo, and now, apparently, postcards.

My slim mailbox in our shared hallway is usually empty, but something told me to check it when I got home, and I knew immediately I had something from him.

Inside, I get comfy on my sofa and I manage to catch him for a video call before he heads to work.

"Did you really send me a postcard?" I ask when he answers, and a huge smile breaks across his face.

Fuck, I miss that smile.

"Might have done."

"Why?" I lift it to my nose and inhale deeply.

"At Christmas, you said a postcard would have been nice. It felt like a guaranteed way to get in touch with you."

"You went to California, not to war," I laugh, sniffing it again. "It smells like you."

"Sprayed it with my cologne before I posted it."

The way my heart flutters and my toes wiggle is almost embarrassing. It's as if I'm stuck in my teenage crush on him. He's never done cute shit like this before, and neither has anyone else. It's so sweet I could puke and still be happy about it.

We sit like that for a while, two idiots who can't stop smiling, until his eyes flick down to his watch and he breaks the spell.

"I'm sorry we keep missing each other, but I need to head to work."

"That's OK. I need to shower anyway. I'm heading out for dinner with a few instructors tonight."

"Have a great time, you deserve it."

I pin his postcard to my wall with all my most treasured photos. Another postcard arrives the following week. And the week after that. Then another. And another.

Chapter 26
Kayla
Ten Winters Ago / Age Eighteen

IN THE FAR CORNER of the pizzeria terrace, Ryan and I sit tucked away from the crowds, eating lunch in the shade of towering pines. Underneath the table, his hand is pressed between my knees and I wish he'd shift it higher.

"Are you a virgin?" I ask him before quickly biting off a huge mouthful of four cheese pizza. Apparently, now is the moment for my brain to blurt out the question I've been dying to ask.

"Uh, yeah. Are you?"

Relief floods through me, and I nod. He doesn't talk about other girls, but he's cute as hell and sweeter than most of the guys back home. Any girl would be lucky to date him, and if he went to my university, I'd definitely ask him out.

We've gotten more handsy this year, but never had enough time alone together to take things further. The end of December means me we only have a few days left here, and now I feel that pressure more than ever.

He tugs on the end of one of my braids. "Why do you ask?"

A blush creeps into my cheeks. I started this conversation, there's no turning back now. "I've been thinking if we still haven't had sex by next year, then we should make a pact to do it together."

It feels safer to make a long-term suggestion rather than ask for what I really want, which is to lose my virginity, like, yesterday. I was sure he'd have lost his already, and he almost certainly won't wait another year.

"Why not this year?" he whispers, his hand finally slipping up the inside of my thigh. "We're old enough."

"You want to? With me?"

"I kind of always thought it would be you," he says, leaning in to kiss me. "Also, I packed condoms."

My lips press together at the thought of him naked and hard. At the thought of me being naked with, not just any boy, but one I already feel comfortable with.

"Did you?" I whisper against his open mouth. "So you've thought about this?"

He smiles, a little puff of air warming my bottom lip. "Little bit. What do you think? Want to be my first?"

"Yes, but..."

He pulls back and his eyes dart between mine. "There's a *but*?"

If this is how intense it feels just talking about it, I can't even imagine looking at him while he's on top of me.

"Promise this won't change things between us."

"I promise." He says it too fast, like he hasn't really thought about what he's asking of me.

"What if you meet someone else?" I ask him, fully aware it'll happen at some point.

"Well, what if *you* meet someone else?"

"I guess we... don't talk about it?"

"So we stay friends when we go back home, live our lives, come back next winter and do it again." He wiggles his eyebrows. I don't know when that stopped being annoying and started being kind of cute. "Deal?"

"Deal."

When our families head out to welcome in the new year at the annual fireworks display, I squeeze his hand as the first explosion lights up the valley.

The very next day, my wish comes true.

Chapter 27
Ryan

It's been weeks since Kayla and I have found time to talk on the phone, and I finally get it.

She was justified in her concerns. These scraps of time would never amount to any kind of relationship. When I go to bed, she's waking up. When she gets off work, I'm headed to the studio. Lunch is quick for both of us, if I manage to get away at all, and there's not a lot of time for texting during the day.

Sometimes weeks go by with only a few messages, but on a couple of occasions we've caught each other at the right time, in the right mood, and it hasn't taken long for our conversations to turn sexual. Phone sex isn't a patch on the real thing, but I'll take whatever I can get with her.

Kayla is always quick to remind me afterwards it changes nothing between us. We're still friends, we still do our own thing, and we'll still see each other next winter. I'd happily live in the delusion, but she gets a kind of post-nut clarity that brings us back to earth.

There've been a flurry of bookings before the season ends, but I know she has today off, so I call her before I've even gotten out of bed.

She answers from the sofa; her face a little pale, hair pulled up into a messy bun.

"Oh, honey. How is my friend Kayla doing?"

"Disgusting," she groans. "I've barely moved all day."

"I thought you might be a little fragile, judging by the tequila photos."

She covers her face with a pillow and screams into it. "Don't say that word. I am my own worst enemy."

Last night was the final Saturday of the winter season, and she headed to Rico's for a farewell party. Today the chairlifts will stop running, the bars will close, and the instructors and chalet staff head back to wherever they call home.

"What do you have planned now?" I ask her, and she sits up, finishing a nearby glass of water.

"Going back to bed. Ordering pizza for dinner. Might watch A Cinderella Story and really torture myself."

She must have watched it fifty times by now, and I laugh at the memory of her reciting lines. She grabs her pillow, and I watch her trek through her small apartment and slide into bed. Even hungover, she's still so beautiful, and I hate the thought of her feeling shitty while she's alone. If I was there, I'd cook for her, run her a bath, hold her in my arms until she fell asleep.

"I didn't mean today, by the way."

"Huh?"

"What do you have planned now winter is over?"

"Lifts open again in June," she sighs, "but I want to explore as much as I can before then and make sure I have some good biking routes locked in. For now, I just want to be lazy for a bit."

"It'll be good for you to take a break." She keeps her phone held up and burrows deeper under her covers. I do the same, imagining us lying side by side in the same bed. "You look so snuggly. I wish I was there with you."

"Me too."

"Was it a good time? At Rico's?"

"Yeah..." she mumbles, her eyes fluttering closed.

Party girl Kayla is a lot of fun, and I bet she had tonnes of attention last night. She looked stunning in the selfie she sent me before leaving the house, her hair in a high ponytail, dark tank top and jeans hugging every curve. If I'd been in the bar, I'd have been first in line to try to get her attention.

"So did you, uh..."

Fuck's sake. I shouldn't be asking.

"Did I what?"

The rules of our situation mean it's none of my business, and she doesn't have to answer, but I ask anyway.

"Did you go home with anyone?"

"Ryan," she says, her tone a warning.

It's a decade old deal. Don't ask, don't tell. We don't owe each other anything, and bringing it up now is like pulling at a loose thread. We won't be able to put it back together if I unravel it all.

Still, I'm dying to know. Kayla is a sexual person, and if I can't be there to give her what she needs, I don't blame her for going elsewhere.

"It's fine if you did," I tell her. "I'm not mad, just interested. As your friend."

It's a bullshit addendum, but it works.

"Yes, I went home with someone," she whispers, and my cock twitches behind my zipper.

"What happened?"

"Stop it," she groans, burying her face in her pillow. I wish I could reach out and reassure her.

"I'm genuinely curious. I want to know."

She sighs and pulls me back into view. "What do you want to know?"

Fuck.

I expected her to spill it, not make me beg for scraps of information. "Did you go to his place or bring him back to yours?"

"His. A hotel."

"Did you know him before last night?"

"No. He flies home today."

"So you won't see him again?"

"Highly unlikely."

Relief floods through me. I can handle the idea of Kayla and a one-night stand. If she told me it was a local, I'd be booking a ticket for the first flight over. I don't care if that makes me a jealous prick.

"Did you…" The words are on the tip of my tongue, but I can't push them past my teeth. "Sorry. Doesn't matter."

"Did I fuck him? Is that what you want to know?"

"Yeah. Did you?"

"If you're asking, I think you know the answer." She pulls her sleeve over her fist and covers her mouth. My girl isn't usually this shy. Kayla had buckets of confidence in the bedroom, and I want to bring her back to life.

"Was it good?"

Her shoulder lifts a couple of inches, then drops again. "Scratched an itch."

My cock, already half-hard from the sound of her voice, surges to full mast at the thought of her getting off. I slip my hand beneath the waistband of my shorts and give it a firm squeeze, just to take the edge off. It doesn't help.

"Is it weird this is turning me on?"

She gasps and bites her lip. "Is it?"

"Yeah, I'm rock fucking hard."

"Show me."

I pull the phone back, tug down my shorts and let my dick spring free, angling the camera so she can see more of me. She moans softly, rolling to her back.

"Do you want to tell me what happened?"

"Are you gonna touch yourself while I do?" she asks, a flicker of challenge in her voice.

"Is that OK?"

She hums gently, sinking lower under her sheets. "Only if I can too."

Chapter 28

Ryan

Her phone switches hands, and I watch her slip her fingers between her lips, wetting them with her tongue before they disappear out of view. She moans a little, shuffling to find a comfortable position, and I think maybe I should book those flights, anyway. The sooner I get to see her do this to herself, the better.

"How did it start?" I ask, trying to tone down my excitement.

"We chatted in the bar, and he seemed fun, so we kissed outside after everyone left."

"Good kisser?"

"Good enough," she laughs, and that pisses me off.

Kayla is hands down the best woman I've ever kissed. She deserves the best in return, not some average guy who doesn't treat her right. Those kisses should have been mine, and I want them now.

"Then what happened?"

"He invited me back to his place, and I was horny, so I said yes."

I've always loved that Kayla owns her sexual needs. When we're together in the mountains, she loves to whisper things to me in inappropriate places, at times when we can't do anything about it. If something is on her mind, she makes it known. That's how the whole wishlist thing started, and my life is infinitely better for it.

"Did you suck his cock?"

"Ryan!" she scolds.

"What?" I laugh. "I'm invested now. I want to know everything."

"Yes, I did."

"You're so good at that. I bet he loved it. On your knees, or on the bed?"

Her head rolls to one side, squeezing her eyes shut. "On my knees."

"That lucky fucker."

My fingers wrap around the base of my shaft, and I grip tightly, watching her face, wishing I could be there. A flash of a memory gives me an idea.

"Hey, do you remember the time I pulled a chair to the foot of your bed and told you exactly what I wanted to see?"

"Yes," she moans. "I think about that night a lot."

I've thought about it a lot, too. How hot she looked spread out before me, how good she was at following my orders. The power trip of being in control of her pleasure was like nothing else. I boost myself up against the headboard and shove my shorts all the way down.

"I want to see all of you, and I want you to have both hands free. Do you think you could set your phone up somehow so I can watch you play with yourself?"

She's out of her bed in a heartbeat, tossing clothes from the chair in the corner and pulling it to the edge of the bed. She takes a few moments to set me up at a good angle, but I get a magnificent view down the front of her loose shirt while I wait. The glimpse of her tits makes me ease up on my dick in case I come too soon.

"Is that good?" she asks, kneeling on the bed until she's all in frame.

"So good. You're so pretty."

"I'm a mess." She rolls her eyes, and I know she doesn't feel it after last night, but she is always gorgeous to me. Reaching up, she fixes her hair where it's falling loose, and her top rides up, revealing a strip of bare stomach I want to sink my teeth into.

"What now?"

"How's the temperature there? Do you want to take your clothes off?"

"It's pretty hot," she laughs, peeling her top up over her head, leaving her in plain black underwear and no bra. "Can't reveal everything right away though, gotta make you work for it."

"Happy to," I tell her. "Now sit back against the headboard with your hands on your stomach. I want you to imagine I'm sitting right behind you and those hands are my hands."

We've done this a few times in person. Me holding her in my arms, ankles hooked over her legs, her body all mine to play with. I'd spend ages kissing her neck, making her squirm while I stroked everywhere except where she wanted me most.

"Close your eyes and stroke your fingers up and down. Nice and soft and slow. Can you picture it? You and me, just like always."

"Yeah, I wish you were here." She presses her knees together, and I get a sick thrill knowing I'll get to see her part them for me soon. There's something about that moment of her opening up for me that gets me every time. I spit in my palm and spread it around the swollen head of my cock.

"Can you tease those pretty nipples for me? The way I do."

She opens her eyes, licks her fingertips, then watches herself run slow circles around them.

"Did he get to put them in his mouth?" I ask, and when she nods, my cock jerks at the thought of watching this guy do all the things I like to do. I can't tell if it's jealousy or fantasy, but right now it's all I want.

"Pinch them. Hard." She rolls them between her fingers, tugging hard enough to make her wince a little.

"What now?" she sighs.

"Now you put your left hand around your throat and your right hand between your legs."

She squeezes her jaw before finding a comfy spot around her neck. Her breath quickens, then I watch her other fingers slip into her underwear.

"Uh-uh," I scold. "No touching yet. Only on the outside until you make a mess of them. If I see you naked right now, it's over for me."

"Oh God, Ryan," she half-laughs, half-moans, her back arching. I might be making her wait, but she wastes no time gripping herself roughly, hips squirming as she grinds against her palm. My hand matches her rhythm, and I spit on it again, eyes never leaving the screen in my hand.

Kayla twists the fabric around her fingers, tugging her underwear tight and high, so I can see how wet she is, the glossy outline of her pussy showing through the thin fabric.

"You're so fucking sexy," I tell her, stroking harder. "Take them off. Show me your cunt."

She lifts her hips and tosses them aside, planting her feet wide and trailing her fingers through her soaked flesh. I watch for a while, entranced, utterly captivated by this perfect, beautiful, filthy woman.

Every part of my body knows I should be there. When she squirms and aches and begs for me to touch her, I should be able to reach out and give her what she wants.

"I wish that was the head of my cock stroking you. Teasing you. Giving you just the tip."

"I hate when you tease me," she groans.

"Your body says otherwise, sweetheart. I can see you clenching just from me speaking about it."

"Can I touch it more? Please."

"Good girl for asking so nicely. Yes, you can fuck yourself."

Chapter 29

Ryan

Two fingers disappear inside, and Kayla throws her head back, moaning in ecstasy at the relief she must feel.

"After you blew him, did he return the favour?" she nods, rolling her lips over her teeth. "Did he suck your clit the way you like?"

"Only a little."

"What a fucking dumbass. He doesn't know how lucky he was to taste you. Can you taste your fingers for me now? Spread it over your pretty mouth."

She paints her lips, then shoves them in her mouth, moaning and sucking them clean. It's obscene to watch, and I pump harder, wishing it was my cock instead of her fingers.

"Then you fucked him?"

"Uh-huh," she groans, hand reaching back between her legs. "Fuck, Ryan, I'm so wet."

"That's good, baby." My pace quickens along with my heart rate. "Oh god, I wish I could have seen it."

Her breath turns shaky. "Do you really?"

"I don't know," I shrug. "I'd probably hate it in reality, but the idea is so fucking hot. Do you think it's messed up I'm asking about it?"

"No, I like telling you, actually. I just wished it was you."

"I wish it was me, too. So much. When you fucked him, did he stretch you?" From the way she whimpers, I have her answer. "He was big?"

"Yeah."

"That's good. You like that feeling. You deserve to get the things you like, Bunny. Go ahead and add another finger for me."

"Oh god," she groans, tipping her head back, adjusting to the sensation. "Feels so good."

Watching her is heavenly, but I want to see more, want her to feel as good as she can.

"Do you still have your purple toy?" I ask, and she moans, shakily. "I want to see you work it inside yourself. See how good you look getting fucked."

Her eyes widen, and she huffs out a harsh breath, swallowing hard as she stops touching herself. She bends over to reach underneath her bed and with her ass up high, I know I could bury my cock straight inside her.

I can't help but laugh at what she comes back with. We've played with a couple of toys before, but clearly she's levelled up.

"You have a whole box now?"

"There might have been a few additions to the squad," she laughs, lifting the lid and searching through it.

"I'm gonna need a demonstration next winter. I want to sit in that chair and watch you get yourself off with everything in that box, even if it takes all day. Even if you're an overstimulated wreck and think you can't keep going, you will. For me. OK?"

"Jesus, Ryan, fuck yes, we can do that. First on the wishlist."

Eventually, she finds her purple dildo, solid and thick. I watch her squirt lube on the tip, then get back into position at the head of the bed.

"Move closer to the phone. I want to see the look on your face when it fills you."

She scoots down the bed until her feet are on either side of the chair and adjusts the camera angle so I can still see all of her.

"Hey," I say, before she gets started. "Kiss me."

"What?"

"Pick up the phone and kiss me real quick."

Her screen only shows my face, I'm the one getting a private show here, but I'd rather she focus on herself than what I'm doing off camera. Still, if I was there, this is a moment where I'd make her pause for a kiss. Those soft moments before things get intense between us are the ones I love most.

"You're so silly," she laughs, but she does it anyway, smacking her lips against the phone screen and then setting me back down.

"Are you ready, baby?"

"Are *you*?"

"Fully cocked and loaded." That's no lie, I'm not sure I've ever been harder. I angle my phone to show her and the tip leaks with pre-cum. She moans when I smear it around, careful not to reach the point of no return before she does.

Kayla hitches one knee higher, opening up for a better view and I get the perfect angle of her toy plunging in to the hilt. Her moan would wake the neighbours. Shit, it might even wake Cameron if he's not awake already. I don't give a fuck though. I want to hear her get loud.

"I need you," she says, sliding it slowly in and out of her glistening cunt.

"As soon as I can, Bunny, I promise. Go faster."

There's no holding back now, my fist picking up the pace, gripping tightly as she fucks herself for my eyes only.

"Oh Jesus, Kayla. You're so fucking pretty, you know that, right? My pretty, pretty girl."

Calling her *'my girl'* isn't fair on either of us, but it slips out and I love to see the way it affects her. She shifts onto her knees, sinks lower onto her toy, filling every inch. Kayla works her fingers in tight circles over her clit, legs trembling as she struggles to keep herself upright.

"What would you do if you were here?" she asks.

"I'd want to start slow, get on my knees and fuck you slowly with your toy. Watch it fill you until you're aching to come."

"I am! I am aching," she groans, tipping her head back.

"But my cock is so hard right now. I need you so bad, I don't know if I'd be able to hold back. I'd want to grab your hair and bite your neck and get a little rough with you. Fuck you like you're mine. Because you are."

"Oh fuck, Ryan."

She keeps going, but the sound of my wet hand pumping my dick is all I can hear.

"Don't forget to breathe, sweetheart," I tell her, and she lets out a soft laugh. She gets so lost in the moment sometimes. It's a beautiful thing to witness, but the last thing I need is her passing out on me when I'm a million miles away.

"Last night, did you come?"

"Yes."

"Who made you come? You or him?"

"Me," she whines, and I can tell she's getting close. "I did it."

"Pathetic," I groan, my hand stroking faster as I listen to her pretty little noises get louder. "I promise I'll make you come over and over next time I get my hands on you. You won't have to worry about anything. You can lie back and let me take care of you. Keep rubbing your clit for me. Keep stroking your neck, just the way I would."

"Please, Ryan, please," she begs.

"I want to see you come, Kayla. Want to watch you shatter for me. Want to bury my face between your legs when you do so I can taste it and keep you coming over and over. You gonna make a mess for me, my good girl?"

"Yes. Yes. I'm gonna — Oh fuck, Ryan."

Her body tenses, hand working faster as her teeth sink into her lip. Her moans turn to whimpers and panting and shaking.

My eyes squeeze shut and I'm right there, at the foot of her bed, cock in hand, watching her fuck herself. Witnessing her pleasure in its rawest form. White hot pressure shoots from the base of my spine and then I feel it, hot and sticky, covering my stomach.

I want to be there. Want to cover her in cum, spread it around, make a big fucking mess, then take my time cleaning her up. I want to taste her, worship her, devour her.

I want her.

I love her.

Her.

Her.

Her.

Chapter 30
Kayla

Weeks later, I'm still thinking about how heated things got the last time Ryan and I spoke. The memory has me zoning out in the middle of the *supermarché*, or clutching the edge of the kitchen counter, or having to go back to bed for a swift midday orgasm.

Listening to Ryan ask me questions about someone else while I touched myself was insanely hot. Somehow even better than the sex itself, and I haven't been able to stop wondering what he's like with other people. I don't care if it's messed up. We've never been normal when it comes to this stuff.

Seducing him is so easy when we're together in person, one of my favourite games, in fact. All I have to do is pout my lips and flutter my eyelashes at him and he knows what I want.

If that doesn't get the message across, hooking a finger behind his belt buckle does the trick. All methods I can't deploy while he's at the other end of the phone and not here in my bedroom.

Asking for sex in person is one thing, when I know the answer will be yes, but asking him to get me off over the phone is quite another.

"Ryan…" I try to drop my voice and make it sound seductive, but I probably sound tired more than anything.

It's late here, just after lunch in California, and I've been looking forward to our call ever since we discovered he'd have a free afternoon this weekend.

He's been surfing with Cameron this morning, but now he's home alone, chilling on his sofa and eating a burrito he picked up on the way back. It's the kind of casual afternoon I picture us spending together, even if there are limited options for Mexican food in my remote part of the world.

Maybe it's something we'd learn to cook together. I'd get really good at making salsas, he'd order special seasonings online, and we'd walk through town hand in hand on weekends to pick up our supplies.

"Yes, Bunny?" he says, swallowing his food and snapping me out of my fantasy. God, I wish I wouldn't drift off into other worlds like that. It hurts too much to come back.

"I, um..." A fit of nervous giggles bubbles out of me, and on my phone screen, he breaks into a smile.

"What's got you acting all shy?"

Those butterflies in my belly go wild. "I really need to come."

He fakes a shocked gasp, eyes wide in scandal, but I can tell he loves it. "Oh, do you? Why's that then?"

I'm already in bed, snuggled underneath the covers, so I sit up a little, lowering the camera angle so he can tell I'm not wearing anything.

"Been thinking about you all day. Excited to hear your voice."

"Well, that makes two of us, sweetheart. What are you in the mood for?"

I sigh a little, twisting the end of one braid in my free hand. "Can you talk me through it, please?"

"You want me to tell you how to touch yourself, sweet girl?"

"I want you to tell me about your last hook up."

"What do you mean?" he says flatly. Maybe this was a mistake.

"That thing we did last month was fucking hot. Me telling you about that guy. I want to hear about the last time you had sex."

His jaw ticks ever so subtly, and he pokes his tongue against the inside of his cheek, considering.

"OK, I'm down. Let me just..." he gets up from his sofa and I watch him walk the hallway towards his bedroom. "Cam could be back any time."

He closes his door and flops onto his bed, but then gets right back up again.

"Actually, let me go wash my hands. If I get hot sauce on my dick, you'll hear me screaming from all the way over there."

He props his phone up on his nightstand so I can watch him leave, wiggling his hips and blowing me kisses as he goes. Rolling my eyes at his goofing off is an ingrained reaction, but I wish I was there, laying on his bed, waiting for him to come back. I wish I knew his place better, from real memories, not just the glimpses I get when we talk and he moves the camera around.

I wish for a lot of things, but that's all they are. Wishes.

Ryan strips out of his t-shirt on the way back and I swear the smell of his skin floods my nostrils. Memories of my cheek against his chest, only a sheen of sweat between us, falling asleep in post-orgasmic bliss.

"So, what do you want to know?" he asks, collapsing onto his stomach, getting comfy with his chest propped up on a folded pillow.

Oh god, he's going to make me say it out loud.

"You know... What have you been up to? Sexually speaking."

"Hmm, well, honestly, the last time was a little rushed because we had places to be."

"Oh."

He sounds dismissive, and I can't tell if that means it was good or bad sex.

"But there was a time, a few days before that, I keep coming back to it when I jerk off. Want me to tell you about that one?"

What the fuck?

"Sure." I try to play it cool, though I'm starting to feel like this talking about other partners kink doesn't work both ways. It's stupid to assume he only thinks about me when he masturbates. Who is this woman? Or are we talking about multiple here?

"Well," he drawls. "It was different from the kind of sex I usually have with you."

"How so?"

"It was kind of slow, and tender. I really took my time with her, made sure it was unforgettable, you know?"

The tight pull in the pit of my stomach doesn't feel as good as it usually does when we talk like this. It grips at the bottom of my lungs, and breathing in feels hellish. What I thought would make me horny, actually makes me want to rip my skin off.

"Are you dating her?"

He suppresses a laugh. "She wouldn't let me even if I tried."

"Did she like it?"

"Oh yeah, she liked it. Want me to keep going?"

"Mm-hmm."

I fucking hate this.

I should never have asked. Blood whooshes so fast in my ears I can't actually focus on his words. I stare into some middle space past my phone screen, only glancing back when he says something that makes my chest hollow out.

"...so then she begged me to come inside her."

I thought I was the only one he'd done that with.

"It felt so good coming inside her. Claiming her in a way. And then she asked me to keep going, and we stared into each other's eyes until we both came again." I pinch the bridge of my nose, look away and try not to cry. "And I really loved it because I'd never done that with anyone before. Or since."

My head snaps up to see him with his chin in his palm, sporting his best shit-eating grin.

Is he talking about us?

"Ryan, no. Are you being serious?"

"Oh yeah," he says, wiggling his eyebrows. "It was so fucking intense. She's really beautiful too. Most beautiful woman I've ever seen. You'd like her, I think."

"Why aren't you sleeping with other people?"

"The only person I want to sleep with is you." He says it so casually, like I've asked him what he wants to eat for dinner.

"What the fuck? So you're not going to have sex until Christmas?"

"You're worth the wait, Bunny."

"But that's not... we're not together... you can't just change the rules like that. We've been over this so many times."

He shifts to sit up by his headboard, and I grab a nearby t-shirt and pull it on. He's seen me naked countless times, but now it feels too vulnerable.

"I know the deal, and I'm not asking you to change any of that. I'm saying, you play by your rules, I'll play by mine. Waiting hasn't been hard, and it's April already."

Bile churns in my belly. If he's waiting, and I'm not, what kind of monster does that make me?

"I need to go," I tell him, looking away when his face falls.

"I thought we had at least an hour crossover?"

"We do, but I don't feel horny anymore. I need some space to think."

"Kayla, don't go getting it all twisted in your head, talk to me. I wouldn't have told you if you hadn't asked. Do you want me to lie? I can make some shit up if you like?"

"No, I don't think I felt comfortable with it, anyway."

"So we're on the same page, then?"

"About?"

"Me not having sex with anyone else."

"You can fuck whoever you want!" I yell, hoping my upstairs neighbour is already in a deep sleep.

"I will," he shrugs. "Next winter."

Chapter 31

Kayla

RYAN: I'm free on Saturday if you've got time to chat.

KAYLA: Got plans sorry

RYAN: No worries

―ele―

RYAN: How's your week going? Send me some pics!

―ele―

RYAN: Can we talk?

THREE MISSED CALLS: RYAN

RYAN: Please answer me? Kayla?

RYAN: I hate that I fucked this up

RYAN: I miss you

Chapter 32
Kayla

He didn't fuck it up. It would be so easy to pick up the phone and call him, but I freaked out and now I'm in some sort of emotional stand-off with myself. I don't know where we go from here.

If we don't talk between now and winter, it'll be awkward as hell. If we do talk, I worry I'm giving him false hope. Not seeing other people is as good as being in a relationship, and I hate that he made a decision for himself without talking to me first.

At first he texted daily, but now it's every few days, and a fucked up bit of my brain wonders how long it would take from him to stop texting at all. Maybe it would be for the best. We'd be back to normal. No contact until Christmas, just like always.

Talking was fun, but now I'm doomed to spend my days stewing in my apartment like I've cut off a limb.

May is the quietest month of the year, with many local businesses taking a holiday. I've got nothing booked until the end of the month, so I'm spending as much time as possible working on my business plans for the summer. The website is up to date, insurances renewed, my marketing materials are in the tourist office, and social media posts are scheduled.

I'm on top of everything, and having nothing to do has me thinking all kinds of wild thoughts.

My parents suggested a trip home to Edinburgh, but every time I look at flights, I end up typing Los Angeles as the destination instead. Usually I snap my laptop closed and force myself not to think about it, but today I'm apparently intent on sabotaging myself.

All I've ever wanted is this life I've built for myself, to live and work in the mountains full-time. If Ryan could be a part of it too, even better, but I accepted long ago I can only be in charge of my own destiny. If he wanted to be here, he would be here, but his life took him in another direction.

I knew what I wanted, and went for it, but I've never truly considered any alternative. Was it remiss of me to not consider other options? What if I liked L.A. as much as the Alps? Maybe then we could have a chance at being together. if it didn't work, at least I'd feel more confident in my decision.

There's only one flight a week at this time of year, and tickets aren't as expensive as I'd expected. It's also Ryan's birthday next week, a date I've known about for most of my life, but never been able to celebrate with him. I keep picturing a world where we get to be together for birthdays. We buy gifts, go to dinner, do some extra hot stuff in bed.

What if the world where we get to celebrate a birthday is this one?

By the time I've chewed half of my bottom lip off, I'm sick of myself. I fire off a text, and Ryan calls immediately.

"Are you serious? You'll come visit?"

"Yes, but you can't read too much into it. I have a quiet couple of weeks and it would be nice to see you, so... are you free?"

"Shit. I'm right at the end of a production. Can you come at the end of the month?"

"I have a school group coming out for residential that week."

"Fuck," he yells, raking his hand through his hair. "You know what, just come, I'll take time off if I can, and every minute I'm not working

I'll spend with you, OK? Please come. It would be so amazing to see you."

I book the ticket and forward a screenshot of my itinerary. The smiling selfie he sends me afterwards is worth the ticket price alone.

Chapter 33
Kayla

After delays and a short layover in London, it took almost an entire day to fly to L.A.

Cameron picked me up from the airport while Ryan was at work, and I spent the rest of the day in bed, dozing on and off, while I waited for him to get home.

I'm used to flying between Geneva and Edinburgh, but I've never ventured this far, and the combination of jetlag and aeroplane lurgies has left me feeling bone tired. I'm only here for five days. Maybe adjusting to a new time zone isn't even worth it.

Ryan got back late last night, and the hours passed in a blur of lazy sex, talking until he fell asleep, and me squirming half the night trying to shut my brain off. Now, with sunlight peeking through his thin curtains, and a helicopter hovering somewhere outside, I watch with one eye open as he dresses for work.

"I'm so sorry I have to go."

"It's fine," I reassure him, for the hundredth time. I knew what I was letting myself in for. Being in the same room as him is enough, I think. Seeing him get dressed in khaki shorts and a loose fitted shirt is strange. It's a totally different vibe to how he dresses in the mountains, but I like it all the same.

"I'll be done as quickly as I can, and then I'm taking you out tonight."

"You are?"

"Absolutely. I booked a table for eight at a place I think you'll love."

The red dress I've hung in his closet will be perfect. I wasn't sure if I'd get a chance to wear anything fancy, but I brought it just in case.

"Do you have plans today?" he asks.

"No, I might explore a little, catch up on some more sleep."

He crouches beside me, freshly shaven and wearing that same cologne he sprays his postcards with. "I'm so fucking happy you're here, Kayla. You have no idea how hard it is to drag myself away from you right now."

"So stay," I beg, reaching an arm out from underneath the blankets to pull at his clothes. "Bunk off with me."

It's not fair to ask, I know. I'd never ditch a work commitment for him. His mouth finds mine and his kisses taste like toothpaste. I probably taste, and look, like death.

"I wish I could. Did you make a wishlist for your time here?"

"I might have done, but I've scrapped it all for the idea of you tying me to this bedframe."

I roll onto my back, stretch my arms above my head, and let the covers fall from my bare chest when I wrap my hands around the bars of his headboard. His eyes flare, and I keep mine locked on his, lick the length of my two middle fingers and slip them beneath the sheets.

"What are you doing?" he whines.

"What?" I shrug, feigning innocence. "If you're not going to make me come, I guess I'll have to do it myself."

"Oh my god, you're a fucking nightmare and a dream all rolled into one," he says, walking backwards out of the room. "But Cam is out, so make all the noise you want, Bunny."

It's all for show. Once I hear the door close, I roll over and bury my face in his pillow, too tired to get myself there, anyway.

> **Ryan:** I can't stop thinking about you naked in my bed and how much I want to run home and fuck you.
>
> **Ryan:** Makes me so happy knowing you're close by
>
> **Ryan:** Whatever you want tonight, it's yours.

My phone rings as I'm adding the finishing touches to my hair and make-up. I never wear much more than sunscreen and mascara in the mountains, and it's so nice to take my time and make an effort for once.

"Hi, are you almost back? I'm nearly ready."

"Kayla, I'm so sorry."

My heart sinks. I drop onto the end of his bed and try not to look too disappointed.

"We're behind schedule here," he continues. "I'm going as fast as I can, but I won't be back in time for dinner."

"It's OK," I tell him, slipping my shoes off. "I wouldn't have lasted long in these heels, anyway."

His face crumples, and he rubs at his eyes. "You look incredible, and I am such a dick. I promise I'll make it up to you."

"Honestly, it's fine."

"I hate this, but I need to get back. I'll be home as fast as I can, I promise."

There's a knock on Ryan's bedroom door a few minutes later, and Cameron's voice, full of pity, on the other side. "Hey Kayla, can I come in?"

His face lights up when he sees my dress and my hair. It took almost an hour to straighten it, and it was all for nothing.

"Oh, you look so nice."

"Thanks. Unfortunately, Ryan won't be back in time for dinner, so I'm about to change out of all this."

"That's why I'm here. I'm taking you out instead."

"Oh God, no, you don't have to do that." My lip wobbles, and he steps closer, wrapping me in a big hug.

"I'm sorry, I know it fucking sucks," he says, holding me tight. "But you came all this way, and he booked a table at Yvet. It would be a crime for you to go home without eating their grilled peach salad."

"Honestly, it's fine," I sniff. "I feel wildly overdressed, anyway."

"Nobody who says they're fine is every actually fine." He releases me and gives my shoulders a friendly squeeze. "Please don't cry. And do not take that dress off. You're gonna fit right in. Give me fifteen minutes to shower and change, and then we're going to eat everything on the menu on Ryan's dime."

Chapter 34
Kayla

Turns out Yvet is the type of restaurant where a red silk dress and four-inch heels actually feels under-dressed, somehow. I've never been anywhere this fancy in my life, all white stone walls, dim lighting, and huge olive trees growing straight out of the floor. The second we walk in from the busy street, I feel transported to somewhere in the Mediterranean.

Our hostess looks like she stepped off of a movie set, and I feel so out of place as she shows us to our table. It's tucked away in a nook that would be romantic were I here with Ryan and not his best friend. The white linen tablecloth is set with polished cutlery, and crisp, thin wine glasses I know probably cost more than a hundred dollars each.

Cameron is a true gentleman, pulling back my chair for me to sit down, and he looks great in cream trousers and a black shirt, his curls styled away from his face. Hannah's a lucky girl. He's certainly not difficult to look at, but neither is anyone else in this restaurant.

"Is that George Clooney?" I whisper, cocking my head to the left. He subtly glances across the room while taking his own seat.

"Sure is."

I force myself to stare at my plate. "How do you not get star-struck coming to places like this?"

"Oh trust me, we do, but we have fantastic poker faces from being around famous people on productions. Also, we don't really come to restaurants like this. Tonight is a special night."

When a server appears to take our order, I let Cameron choose for us both. It's a small plates situation, and such decisions feel too overwhelming under these circumstances. He asks for a bottle of champagne, and when it arrives, the first sip is so delicious, I finally start to relax a little.

"So, what's it like living in L.A.?" I ask him, unsure how to make small talk even though I do it almost every day at work. Meeting people from all over the world and asking them to trust you with their safety means you have to find common ground and put them at ease quickly. I'm clearly losing my touch in the off season.

"I mean, I grew up here, so I don't know any different, but I've always loved it. The sun, the surfing, the opportunities. I love working in the film industry, and if that's your thing, there's nowhere better."

That hits a little too hard, given I know how much this industry means to Ryan, too.

"And what about your... other work?" I ask discreetly. Cameron blushes and tries to hide it with a swig of champagne. "Sorry, I didn't mean to embarrass you."

"No, I just wasn't sure how much you know about it."

Turns out there's no easy way to talk about audio porn in public. "Let's say I'm familiar with the genre, but not a consumer of your particular, um, output."

"Understood," he says, and we both burst out laughing.

We dance around the actual content of his work, but he tells me how his subscriber numbers are up, and he's aiming to reach a point where he can turn audios into a full-time job by the end of the year. I love to meet people who've found their calling.

So often my clients talk about how they wish they could live in the mountains, but their real lives are holding them back. It makes me feel so lucky to have found my *thing,* and be able to turn it into a career too. I'd have a very hard time trying anything else, and, so far, this trip is cementing that feeling.

When our food arrives, we tuck into several dishes, passing them back and forth across the table. He was right, the grilled peach salad is amazing, but so is the charred zucchini with white bean mash, the ricotta ravioli, and the lemon zest crispy potatoes.

"And how are things with Hannah?" I ask.

He breaks into a wide smile, the corners of his eyes crinkling at the mention of her name. I wonder what Ryan's face looks like when my name comes up in conversation. If he talks about me at all.

"They're so great. I mean, I miss her loads, but we talk most days."

"That's good. Long-distance relationships are hard work."

"They are, but I'm actually…" he leans in and lowers his voice. "Hannah doesn't know this yet, but I've applied for a sound job in London. If I get it, I'll be able to move there as soon as I can."

"Wow, Cameron, that's amazing. I'm keeping everything crossed for you."

I nod along while he talks me through his vision about how it will all play out, the room blurring around me. Cameron reaches across the table for my hand.

"Hey, don't cry. Did I say something wrong?"

"No, definitely not. I'm thrilled for you."

"What's going on?"

I pat my tears with my napkin, hoping I haven't smudged my makeup too badly.

"Is it really that easy?" From the look on his face, he doesn't follow. "You love her, so you pack up your life and go be with her?"

"Well, yeah," he says with a lopsided smile. "She's settled in London, loves being close to her parents. It doesn't make any sense for her to come here, and I'd do anything for my girl."

Pressing my fingertips into the corners of my eyes does nothing to stem the flow of tears.

"Does Ryan know you're going?" I ask him, and he shakes his head.

"I don't want to say anything until I know for sure. Can you keep my secret?" He holds his pinkie finger out across the table, and I hook mine around it and shake.

"My lips are sealed."

"How are you guys finding the whole long distance relationship thing?" Cameron asks, taking a forkful of ravioli while I almost choke on mine.

"Well, it's different. We're not in a relationship."

"Oh," he says, leaning back in his chair. "I'm sorry. With the way he talks, and you being here right now. I thought… I thought you were giving it a shot."

"What does he say?"

He narrows his eyes, leaning in with a smirk. "You gonna make me break bro-code?"

"He really talks about me?"

"Only every time I see him. He really cares about you, Kayla."

When I thought about this trip, I pictured sunshine and beaches, goofy selfies in front of the Hollywood sign. I didn't picture me in heels I can barely walk in, sobbing behind a napkin in a restaurant full of celebrities, with Ryan nowhere to be seen.

"I'm so confused, Cam. We've always done this whole *'see you next winter'* thing. I'm a temporary person in his life. We've never met up outside the mountains, never even kept in touch until this year. I don't know what the fuck I'm doing here, to be honest."

It's the first time I've expressed those feelings to anyone else, and the relief of having it out there is palpable.

"I don't know what happened last Christmas, but something changed for sure. He's down bad, and he hates himself for not being here tonight. But..." he says, topping up our drinks. "He's just a guy."

His warm laugh reminds me of what my girlfriends back in Edinburgh would probably say if they could see me right now. Nobody even knows I'm here, except Ryan and Cameron. I'm always fixated on him keeping me a secret, when that's exactly what I'm doing.

"And..." Cam continues, raising his glass to clink with mine. "We're not going to let some dumb boy put us off dessert now, are we?"

I hide my giggles behind my palm while we toast. "Nope."

"Cheers to that!"

Chapter 35
Ryan

Traffic is crazy busy at this time of night, and I make it to Yvet just as Cameron and Kayla are leaving the restaurant arm in arm. They're joking and laughing like old friends, but the way her face falls when she sees me is going to haunt me for a long, long time.

"Thanks, man."

"My pleasure," Cameron says, eyes twinkling as he releases Kayla from his crooked elbow. "We've had a blast, right?"

"We have," she says, smiling up at him.

"I am so sorry I couldn't make it," I tell her again, but I'm sick of hearing myself say it, and I'm sure she is too. "It's not too late. Do you want to go for a drink somewhere?"

She rubs her belly. "I'm exhausted, and so full from dinner. Can we go back to your place?"

"Sure, of course. Anything you want."

Beside us, Cameron pulls out his phone. "Some friends are having drinks nearby, so I'll leave you guys to it."

I don't know if that's true or not, but I appreciate the gesture. Some alone time will hopefully get us back on track.

"Thank you for dinner, Cam. I had a really nice night."

Kayla hugs him goodbye, and I shake his hand, then take hers and weave our fingers together. The tips are painted a glossy red to match her dress. She made a lot of effort for this dinner, and I fucked up big time.

Back at the apartment, she kicks off her heels the second we're through the door, groaning in relief. I hang up my jacket and run my hands up and down the sides of her waist.

Her dress really is stunning. Long, and deep red, made of silky fabric that hugs her curves and pools at her chest. We stay like that for a while, my hands roaming, craving all of her in the darkness of my hallway.

"You wore this to dinner with my best friend?" I tease, hooking a finger underneath the delicate straps on her shoulder.

Kayla scoffs, then pokes me hard in the sternum with one finger. "I wore it to dinner with you, you asshole. It's not my fault you didn't show up."

"Well, I'm here now, and so fucking lucky I'm the one who gets to help you out of it."

I wrap my arms around her waist, pulling her tight to me and walking her backwards to my bedroom.

"So beautiful," I murmur against her neck on the way. "This beautiful back, your beautiful hips."

She tips her head to one side, giving me space to run my lips softly along the column of her throat. I could do this for hours, explore her body, the scent of her skin, the taste of it all.

At the foot of my bed, her mouth finds mine, and she opens on a moan, letting my tongue sweep into hers. Kayla closes her eyes, her hands clutching at my sides while I take it slow, revisiting old memories, making new ones with every nip of her lips.

When she tears her mouth away, she drops to her knees in front of me, and makes light work of my belt buckle and zipper. My stomach twists uncomfortably.

"Stop," I whisper, covering her hand with mine. "I don't—"

She looks up at me, her head cocked to one side. "Since when don't you want to get your dick sucked?"

"Since we're not in a hurry," I tell her, pulling her to her feet. "Since kissing you is my favourite thing to do.

"I don't want to kiss," she says, unzipping her dress and slipping it off her shoulders. It falls to the floor, and I feel robbed of the chance to undress her myself. She kicks it to one side and lays back on my bed, a vision in black lace underwear I've never seen before.

Reaching behind her back, she unclasps her bra and tosses it aside, then shimmies out of her panties and sends those flying too.

"Just fuck me rough, OK?"

I hear the words, but I can't make my body react to them.

"I... I..."

"You don't want to fuck me?" she asks, trailing her fingers down between her breasts. "I made myself all pretty for you so you can ruin my make-up."

"I do, I just..." *Oh God, I do, but not like this.* "I'm not... I want to take my time with you. Enjoy every second."

Kayla swallows hard and sits up. She lifts her knees to her chest and presses her fingertips against her eye sockets. When I reach out to stroke her hair, so long and soft with how she's straightened it, she ducks away.

"It's been a long day," she says, taking a deep breath. "Can you pass me a t-shirt?"

My heart is racing as I fetch one of mine from the closet. She turns away to pull it over her head and starts rummaging in her luggage.

"Did I say something wrong?" I ask.

"My body clock is still on French time, I think. It's so late, I think I want to take my make-up off and go to sleep." She finds what she's looking for, squirting some lotion onto a cotton pad and sweeping it over her eyes.

"Kayla, I'm sorry, I couldn't help it. Please don't be mad."

"I know you couldn't," she says brightly, but I can tell it's forced. "I'm not mad at you, I'm just—"

"Oh fuck. Please don't say you're disappointed."

"Well, I am," she snaps, spinning to face me and throwing her hands in the air. "I knew you'd be working, I knew I'd hate being in a city, and I don't know what I was thinking, coming out here like this."

"I'm sorry, OK?" I slump onto the foot of my bed, my head in my hands. "I'm so fucking sorry, but I can't just leave work. It's not that kind of job."

We never fight, so we switch to heavy sighs and words pulled back from the brink of being spoken aloud. When she's done removing her make-up in silence, she stands in front of me and pulls my head to her stomach. Her fingers weave through the strands of my hair and she holds me there while we calm down.

"I'm sorry, too," she says softly. "I knew what I was getting into, and it's not fair of me to put that on you. I probably should have waited until the timing was better but I really wanted to see you. We've never had a birthday together, and I wanted to be here for that."

My hands cup the backs of her legs, smooth and firm, grounding me to the one thing I've always found comfort in. Her.

"I wanted to see you, too. I'd shrink you down and take you to work in my pocket if I could."

She giggles at the thought, letting go and crawling underneath the covers.

"We should get some sleep."

Our bodies shift until we find a comfy position with me behind her. Kayla reaches back for my arm and pushes my hand up underneath her shirt to rest over her heart. In minutes, she's snoring softly in my arms, the way I wish for every night.

I'm not a praying man, but I don't know who else to ask now. I let my eyes drift close, and whisper against her hair.

"If there's a world where this works, please God let it be this one. I can't lose her."

Chapter 36
Kayla

I MANAGE A COUPLE of hours of sleep, but Ryan tosses and turns all night. Getting out of bed before six feels illegal, so I force myself to stay beside him, watching until the clock on my phone ticks over into the next hour.

Carefully, I slip out of his sheets and into the shared bathroom across the hall. The water pressure is good, thank god, and I scrub my skin pink, while silent tears slip down the drain.

This was supposed to be a fun trip. I don't understand how being here can hurt so much. How one person can be both a blessing and a curse? I hate that I fell for someone I'll never be able to have in all the ways I want.

After drying off, I make a fresh pot of coffee and curl up on his sofa with my book. On Saturday mornings at home, I like to get out as early as possible, but right now there's nothing that appeals more than this.

Ryan appears a few hours later, his blankets wrapped around his shoulders like on nights we stayed up late to watch movies in our Christmas PJs. In hindsight, it was an easy ploy to distract us so our parents could eat dinner together in peace, but at the time we three kids felt like it was a treat for us.

"Did you sleep here?" he asks, rubbing his tired eyes.

"No, I woke up early and didn't want to disturb you." Nobody benefits from me telling him I lay awake for hours.

"I hate waking up without you."

He crawls onto the sofa, curling underneath his blankets until his head is in my lap.

Home.

"Are we OK?" he asks. It's a question that feels impossible for us to answer.

My thumb strokes his temple and his hand wraps around my back, sneaking underneath my t-shirt to find a patch of bare skin. Honestly, I don't know what OK looks like for us, but I think we're going round in circles. I don't want to ruin the rest of our time together.

"Do you need to work today?" I ask him, hoping it won't start another fight.

"I'm off today and tomorrow. I'll start late on Monday so I can take you to the airport."

"OK, so what do you want to do today?"

"I have two options in my head," he says, yawning in my lap. "It's a nice day. We can take a drive up into the hills, find a quiet spot, maybe take a little walk. Or we can go to Trader Joe's and buy a bunch of fun snacks and come back and watch movies in bed."

"Oh," I laugh. "I for sure thought one of those options was going to be sexual."

"Sweetheart, I love having sex with you. I'd make it my full-time job if I could, but I love being with you more. All I want is for you to be happy."

"I want the snacks," I tell him, and he lifts my t-shirt to kiss my stomach.

"Then we'll get the snacks."

"And I'm picking the movies."

"Of course you are," he says, kissing me again.

"And we're watching them naked."

And again. "Deal."

When his clock ticks past midnight, we're tangled in his bedsheets, hopped up on sugar, ignoring the movie in the background. I wish him a happy birthday, and kiss him so hard I hope he'll remember this one over all the others.

Chapter 37
Kayla

L.A. WAS A STUPID idea. All I got was a broken heart and an addiction to Red Vines.

Did I think I would fall in love with the place and make plans to abandon my life in the mountains? Obviously not. Would I see a side of Ryan that was all icks and come back wondering what I have ever seen in him? Despite our limited time together, that was never going to happen.

I used to wake up so excited for the day ahead, now I'm cursing the mountain, and time-zones, and my stupid, stupid heart before I've even opened my eyes. My whole life I've wanted this, now I'm mad at myself for even considering giving it a try because now I'm in so fucking deep with this boy.

He snuck one of his hoodies into my suitcase before I left, and I've slipped it over a pillow to snuggle up with at night. Breathing in the scent of his skin and his hair gel, I sleep more deeply than I ever do alone.

Chapter 38
Kayla
Eleven Winters Ago / Age Seventeen

RYAN SITS ON THE lip of a snowbank, rummaging in his backpack for the chocolate spread sandwiches he made before leaving his house this morning. Once I've jammed my skis and poles into the snow, I drop my helmet next to his and sit behind him.

The back of his jacket is warm from the midday sun, and I rest my cheek against it, then pull at his collar so I can kiss the skin at the nape of his neck. He hums and a shudder rolls down his spine.

"Here's your sandwich," he says, passing it back over his shoulder. I take it, then rub my nose against the back of his head and inhale deeply.

"Did you just sniff me?"

"I really like your hair gel," I tell him, raking my fingers through the tufts his helmet has ruffled up. I still can't believe I get to touch him like this, though my spidey senses are on alert in case one of our parents skis past our chosen picnic spot.

"That's weird."

"No, what's weird is opening pots of it in the supermarket back home so I can remember what you smell like."

"You are such a freak," he teases, grabbing my thighs and pulling them tighter around his waist.

I yelp and throw my body back into the snow. "Careful! You'll tip us over the edge. I'm not ready to die."

"At least we'd die happy," he says, leaning back so his head rests on my stomach.

In these stolen pockets of time, my thoughts run away with me. "I wish we could live here all the time."

He makes a satisfied humming noise. "What would we do?"

"I'd like to teach skiing, I think. Maybe guided touring."

"You'd be so good at that, but what about summer?"

"Bikes. Walking. Swimming in the lakes. Beers. Barbecues. Suntans."

"Sounds like a pretty good life to me," he says, rolling over and pressing himself up to kiss me.

Four days later, I'm back home in Edinburgh, sobbing my way through unpacking. When I pull my half-zip fleece out of my suitcase, something falls to the floor and rolls under the bed. I drop to my knees and scramble about for it, but I know what it is as soon as my palm wraps around the hard plastic container.

Twisting open the cap, more tears come when I press my nose to it. It smells like green apples, mountain air, and Ryan's hair.

Chapter 39
Ryan

CAMERON MOVED OUT IN early June, and though I should have seen it coming, it was still a shock. It's been real quiet around here ever since, and as nice as it would be to split the rent, I don't have the time, energy, or motivation to hunt for another roommate.

I'm almost certain I'd never find another one like him, even if I think he's a dick for falling in love with my sister and ditching me for her.

There isn't much time to dwell on it while I'm working long days on a new sci-fi series. It's been a few years since I worked on this genre, and I enjoy the technical challenge, but my whole life feels like it's spent working, eating, sleeping, and trying to catch Kayla whenever I can. One more month and I'll be able to find some time for myself again.

"You missing Cam?" she asks, her phone propped up on her kitchen counter while she gets ready for a day of work.

"Missing you more," I tell her, and she pokes her tongue out at the camera. The topic of us as a couple is strictly off-limits, another unspoken rule I'm doing my best to uphold. Ever since she flew out to see me, our conversations are light and playful, with a sprinkling of filth if we find a convenient time.

"You should visit him when this production wraps, have a few days at home. You haven't taken a break all year."

"You're one to talk, Miss Climbing Mountains Seven Days A Week."

"That's my business, Ryan, and my job doesn't feel like work, so it's fine."

There was a time where mine didn't feel like work either. When I was fresh-faced in Hollywood and hungry for all the experience I could get. Most people don't think about the work that goes into making a film or TV show sound good, but I loved being part of a team that makes all it come together. I still get a thrill seeing the final cut and my name in credits, but now I'm approaching my thirties with a backache from sitting at a desk in a dark room most days.

"Where are you trekking today?"

"Up to The Marmot. We'll stop there for an early lunch, then carry on to the peak."

We spent a couple of summers in the chalet when we were kids, but I've never seen the peaks at this time of year. Not the way Kayla has.

Rolling onto my back, I stare up at the dated cream popcorn ceiling of my tiny apartment. The walls are the same colour and they feel like they're closing in on me. There's no life in this place. No personality. No Kayla.

Wishing she was here is pointless. She hated it.

"I wish I was coming with you."

"Well, what if you..." she trails off, and I see her shake away the thought while adding protein bars to her day pack.

"What if I what?"

"I was thinking if you do go visit Hannah and Cameron, maybe you could fly out here for a couple of days. See what summer in the Alps has to offer."

The only thing I'd want to see is you.

"Are you asking me to visit?" I tease.

When she flew back last month, we said goodbye as if it would be another six months before I saw her again. She doesn't think we can make this work, but I haven't given up hope yet.

"You don't need my invitation or permission. I'm sure your parents would let you stay at their house."

"Oh, I wouldn't get to stay with you?"

"No way, you'll be too much of a distraction."

"But our house is booked out all summer," I protest.

"Oh, well," she shrugs. "Hotel it is."

"So what, I'd have to sneak into your apartment like I used to at the chalet?"

Kayla's family chalet has two balconies running the length of the house, one across the first floor where the living areas are, another on the top floor where patio doors open out from the back bedrooms. Steps up the side of the house give access to the middle and upper floors, and when we were younger, we were always sneaking in and out of her house this way.

Once I misjudged it, and when her dad flicked on his bedroom lights, I had to see him naked, then drop to the floor and crawl the rest of the way to her room.

"Mm-hm," she sighs, lost in her own memories. "And maybe you'll wear a mask this time?"

The idea of it makes me burst out laughing. "A mask?"

"Yeah, like a ski mask or a hockey mask. Ooh! Or the one from Scream!"

"What the fuck? You sicko."

"Dude, don't yuck my yum. I think it's pretty hot," she says, swiping a smear of lip-gloss on in her hallway mirror. "A sexy intruder, but one you know isn't going to murder you while you sleep. We could tussle a little, but I'd let you win in the end."

"Did you get this idea from a book?" I ask, and I can imagine how warm her laugh would feel against my cheek if we were having this conversation in person.

"Maybe. Like you wouldn't be into slipping between my bedsheets and waking me up with your boner."

My cock pulses at the thought of it. It's pretty kinky, but Kayla and I will give most stuff a try, and we didn't have time to do any kind of roleplay when she was here. I slip my hand into my boxer briefs and stroke it gently, feeling it thicken in my hand.

Kayla's put plenty of ideas from her romance books on her bedroom wishlists in the past. We're no strangers to rough sex, and we've had a lot of fun taking turns to be in control. If she wants me to sneak into her bedroom, who am I to object? I'm so far gone for this girl, I'd do basically anything she asked for at this point.

"Only if you let me cover your mouth."

"Mmmm. Shame there's no way of doing that at my apartment," Kayla says, then throws her head back and groans loudly. "Stop making me horny. I'm trying to go to work."

"You stop making *me* horny. I was trying to sleep before you called."

"Bullshit," she says, slipping her coat on and unlocking the door to her apartment. "Your dick is already in your hand and if you tell me it's not, you're a huge liar."

Chapter 40
Ryan

Cameron welcomes me into their London flat with open arms, and I realise that, apart from my pat-down by airport security, this is the first physical contact I've had with another human since he moved out. Not ready to let go, I hold him a little tighter, and he hugs me right back.

"Thanks for letting me stay. I know it's a little last minute."

One series wrapped just as another got delayed, leaving me with a free week that made absolute sense to take as a vacation.

Kayla was right, as always. I've had my head down for months, spending countless hours hidden away in a dark studio. What's the point of making a living if you don't have any time to do something with it?

Cameron closes the door behind me and takes my bags, welcoming me inside.

"It's fine, man. It's so good to see you. Welcome to our house of fun," he jokes. They've lived here together for a while now, but the place has all the markings of my sister's minimalist style.

"Dude, you live with Hannah. I've met her, I know she's the opposite of fun to live with."

"Hey, that's my girl you're talking about," he scolds. "And I'm having a lot of fun living with her."

He pumps his eyebrows, and I pretend to puke. "I know I don't need to remind you that's my sister, you're talking about."

"What are you gonna do, try to kick my ass again?" he laughs. We've more than cleared the air on the incident at Christmas, but I know he'll probably rib me about it for the rest of my life.

Cameron leads me through to their guest bedroom, which also doubles up as his home studio. The walls are covered with acoustic foam panels, and his desk is set up with an array of microphones and screens. His set-up is a lot fancier than it was back home.

"So I got you towels, and an extra pillow. There's an adapter here if you only have your US charger," he says, but I'm too busy looking at the bookcase which doesn't contain a single book.

Instead, it's stacked with more sex toys than I've ever seen in my life. Dildos and vibrators, paddles and floggers, and what looks like a bulk case of lube.

"That's all work stuff," he says, gripping my shoulders and steering me away. "I promise I haven't used it on your sister."

I smack his hand away. "What the fuck, Cam? That's not even where my brain went, you dick."

When I asked if I could crash in their spare room for a couple of nights, it hadn't occurred to me it's also the room where Cam records audio of him jerking off. I know a little more about how Cameron produces his work now, but I don't need to sleep next to a million visual reminders.

"You want to have a beer and pretend I never said anything?"

"Sure," I nod, and I head through to the living room while he grabs two from the kitchen. It's the same brand Kayla likes, and as the first sip coats my throat, I picture her tipping her head back and doing the same. The long line of her neck, the little snowflake necklace that sits at her collarbone.

Fuck, I miss that neck. Kissing her there, nipping her skin, sucking hard enough to leave a mark. It's wild to think I'll get to see her in just a couple of days.

Cam settles into one end of their sofa, but I'm too antsy to sit, and opt for pacing instead. A vase of fresh flowers sits on their dining table, and that's the stuff I wish I could do for Kayla.

Along one wall, Hannah has a bunch of framed photos on display, including some cute ones of the two of them together last Christmas, selfies they must have taken when I wasn't around. It's annoying how good they look together. My gaze lands on one Dad took of the four of us posing with a couple of the Elves at the parade. My arm is around Kayla's shoulder, hers is around my waist, and while Cam and Hannah are looking at the camera, we're only looking at each other.

I need a copy of this photo.

"So you're happy here, London Boy?"

"Sure am. I'm on a job at Pinewood, but once that's over, I think I'll make the switch to working on *Mac'n'Please* full time."

"That's great, man. I'm really pleased you're making so much money from wanking."

"Anyone can do it," he laughs. "What do you have planned for while you're here?"

"Honestly, I haven't made plans. A couple of days to catch up with you guys and my parents before I fly out to see Kayla."

"How's she doing?" he asks.

"She's good," I say, avoiding his gaze. In theory, it's true, she's absolutely fine, but I know now, while we're apart, we'll never be fine. There'll always be something missing. At least that's how it is for me.

Now I'm here in London, it feels insane to be so much closer, and still so far apart. She's not expecting me until Saturday, but that's two whole days without my girl, in a year where we've already spent most of it apart.

When Hannah gets home from work an hour later, her arms are full of bags of takeout from a nearby Thai restaurant they love. Cam and I set everything out on the table while she changes out of her work clothes into something more casual.

It's still weird as fuck to see my sister and my best friend living together, doing all this cute shit like serving up food, and kissing in the kitchen. He tells her he loves her, and she says it right back. There's no hiding, no shame, not an ounce of uncertainty when they look at each other. That's what I want with Kayla. What I've always wanted.

The food smells delicious, but every mouthful is an effort to swallow. I don't know whether it's jetlag, or witnessing their domestic bliss, or the anticipation, but I can't relax. The longer it goes on, the more I feel like I can't breathe.

"Are you OK?" Hannah asks, nudging me with her foot. "Why aren't you yapping?"

I can't do this. Can't sit here and make small talk and act like everything is fine when I could be in the mountains.

"I need to go."

"Where?"

"Airport," I mumble, pulling up my Uber app to book a car.

"You're not serious? You just got here."

"I can't fucking think straight, I need to see her tonight." I stand, then feel light-headed and sit again. Am I really doing this? "Fuck, I don't know which airport has the next flight to Geneva."

"City has a flight in ninety minutes," Cameron chimes in, and when we both whip our heads to look at him, he laughs and shrugs. "What? I knew the second he arrived, he wouldn't make it through the night."

I cup his face and smack a kiss on his cheek. "You're the second best person in the world, you know that?"

"I'd better be first," Hannah huffs.

"Kayla is first," Cameron and I both answer at the same time.

"Fine," she sighs, reaching for the food on my plate. "I'm not one to stand in the way of love, especially if it means more prawn toast for me. You book the flight, I'll book the Uber."

Chapter 41
Ryan

Booking spontaneous flights from Los Angeles to Geneva last Christmas felt pretty outrageous, but this feels even crazier. My knee has barely stopped jiggling the entire flight, all my nervous anticipation desperately seeking a way out. I don't think I'll feel settled until I'm back in her arms.

My luggage is first off the plane, the security gods look fondly on me, and soon I'm in a hire car and on the road. I could have waited for a shuttle bus, but those take forever on the winding roads and I need to see her now.

As luck would have it, Kayla is staying at her parents' house while they have some maintenance work done before the high season, and I plan to take full advantage of having the place to ourselves every night. She's not expecting me for another two days, so I have to hope she's home and I don't have to chase her all over the mountain.

When I turn onto the road up to our houses, I spot her, those unmistakable blonde braids, walking up from town with some fucking guy by her side. When they pass underneath a streetlamp, I see she's in a summer dress, the skirt swishing around her bare legs, and I nearly lose my mind at the thought of running my hands up underneath them and finding her wet and aching for me.

Overtaking them, I pull over and park across the street from my place. It's far enough up the hill she won't notice me, close enough I can still watch her like some fucking creep.

They stroll up the hill and pause outside the front steps to her chalet. In my rearview mirror, I watch him put his hand on her shoulder, and I don't fucking like it.

Despite my best efforts, she's made it clear we're not in a relationship. Whatever she does with her time around our visits is up to her, but if she sends me away, I don't know if I'll get over it.

She's right there, close enough to reach out and grab, and my head is so twisted up over her I can't think straight. I need her touch to ground me.

If she invites him inside, the surprise will be ruined, but I came all this way for her, for *my* girl, and I'm not about to let some other guy take her home.

I take it as a good sign they're still in the street. While she's busy talking to this douchebag, I grab my backpack from the passenger seat, step out quietly, and cross the road.

Sneaking around the back of my family's chalet, I desperately hope I don't interrupt this week's guests. The lights are off, but you never know who might be sitting out on the back patio or relaxing in the hot tub. Thankfully, all is quiet, so I hop up the grassy bank at the back of the garden and make my way down to Kayla's house.

In winter, this is all hidden by snow and it takes a couple of minutes to crunch my way over. Now it's all flat grass, and I'm climbing the steps to her balcony before I know it.

Her parents were always telling her off for forgetting to lock her door to the outside, and when I chance my luck, there's no resistance in the handle.

Jackpot.

She'll get an earful for that later, but for now I slip inside, and wait with my ear beside the gap in the door to the main house. When I hear the front door open, then close, I pray for one set of footsteps, not two.

In the silence of her bedroom, my breathing kicks up a notch. This is a fucking stupid idea. What if she brings this guy inside, up to her room, and I'm here waiting? Am I going to jump into her closet and be subjected to whatever unfolds, or will I have to sit on the end of her bed like a chump and explain myself.

Or will she come up here alone, and I can surprise her by making her sexy intruder fantasy come true?

Now I'm here, I can't see it playing out well for me. Kayla is fucking strong. She might have been the one to plant the idea of me breaking into her bedroom, but she'll probably knock me out before I even get a word in.

A ski mask is so impractical for the middle of summer, but it was a big part of the rush for her, so I dig it out of my bag and pull it over my head, anyway. In the mirror, I give myself a jumpscare. If I found a guy like this in my bedroom, I'd shit my pants and dive out of the window.

With my back plastered to the wall, I listen for voices, but all I hear is Kayla singing to herself and tidying up in the kitchen. After a few minutes she climbs the stairs to this floor, not skipping the third and fifth ones that creak. Why would she? I'm the one sneaking around, not her.

The sound of my blood thumping in my ears makes it hard to focus on her next steps. I can't tell if she's headed for the bathroom or the—

"Oof!"

Her bedroom door hits me in the face as she barges through it and I move fast, grabbing her from behind and pinning her arms to the side. As predicted, she puts up a good fight, kicking me in the leg and throwing her head back to headbutt my nose. Luckily, I saw that one coming and duck to one side, lifting her off the ground to get her under control. She tries to scream, and I clasp my hand over her mouth to silence her.

"Easy now, Bunny," I whisper close to her ear, and though she softens in my arms the second she recognises my voice, I can still feel the adrenaline coursing through her body. Her chest heaves, and when she tries to squirm out of my hold again, I know this time it's all for show.

"Sh-shhh. Sexy intruder, remember?"

She moans, tipping her head back against my shoulder. I dip mine to look right at her, needing to check she's still as into this idea as she was when she first mentioned it. She moans when she sees the mask, fast breaths huffing in and out of her nose.

"Is that a yes? You still want that?"

She nods behind my hand, pressing a kiss to the middle of my palm. I take a deep breath and get into character.

"I'm gonna let go of your mouth now," I growl against her ear, "But if you scream again, I will fill it with my cock so fucking fast. Do you understand me?"

She nods again and I drag my hand lower, feeling her pulse flutter in her neck while she gulps down air.

"Who's the guy?"

"Matty. He leads bike tours."

"He mean something to you?" I ask, and she quickly shakes her head.

"Just a friend."

The way he kept putting his hand on her didn't look friendly to me. "Does he know that?"

"Probably not," she laughs, making my cock throb. I love it when Kayla leans into her bratty side. The thought of another man thinking he can have a chance with her pisses me off enough to spur me on.

"What a little cocktease you are. Did you kiss him?"

"No."

I spin her to face me and grip her jaw between my thumb and fingers. There's a brief flash of panic in her eyes, but it gives way to a look I'm much more familiar with. Lust.

That look betrays her. She's not scared, and she has no reason to be. No, she's excited. Kayla knows I'd never hurt her. I live to give her everything she craves.

Her chest heaves close between us, tits full and high in her strappy sundress. Her skin is golden from her days outside in the summer sun, freckles dusting the tops of her shoulders.

"You'd better not be lying to me, Bunny. When I put my tongue in your mouth, the only thing I want to taste is you."

"I'm not lying." She opens her mouth and sticks out her tongue, spurring me on.

I dip my head and slowly lick the length of it, staring into her eyes the entire time. She tastes of salt and beer and her, but when she leans in to kiss me, I pull away.

"How much have you had to drink?"

She holds up two fingers. I snatch them in my fist and bring them to my mouth, sucking them deep. She whimpers as she watches me, and her hips tip forward, grinding against the rock solid erection that threatens to bust out of my shorts.

I spit on her fingers and flip the skirt part of her dress up, revealing white, lacy panties. I hope she won't mind if I ruin them tonight.

"Touch yourself," I bark at her, and she shoves her hand down the front, groaning at the sensation. It gives me a thrill to know this is turning her on as much as it is me.

Backing her up against the wall, I make space between us, keeping my arm locked with my hand at her throat, holding her gently in place.

"Fuck yourself," I tell her, watching as her hand works faster. With my other hand, I pull the straps of her dress down, tugging it until it gathers at her waist and her tits spill free. Her beautiful chest heaves with each hurried gasp for air.

"I can hear how wet you are, Kayla. Are you my desperate little slut?" Her eyes flare, then roll back in her head. "Spread your legs wider and keep going."

Of all the shit we've done, this is some of the darkest, but she's always been my safe place to explore fantasies, and I've always been hers. We know we'll never hurt each other. This is just a way for the raw animals inside us to come out, the ones that want nothing more than to scratch and bite and suck and fuck.

Kayla shifts her focus to her clit. When her legs begin to tremble, I can tell she's getting close. I release her throat, pinch her tight nipples, and smack them hard. The sensation has her squirming against her hand, and I haul it out of her underwear and up to my mouth.

"Mine," I growl, sucking her fingers clean, then shoving my tongue in her mouth. She opens for me, kissing me back, clutching my t-shirt in her fists and leaping into my arms.

With one hand under her ass, I reach the other between us, tug the damp lace to one side, and thrust two fingers straight into her wet heat. "Were you close, Bunny?"

"Yes," she cries, her head dropping to my shoulder.

"You need to come real bad, don't you?"

Her hips rock back and forth, fucking herself on my hand, desperately seeking pleasure.

"Oh, no you don't."

I pull her away from the wall and carry her across the room.

"On the bed. Face down." She bounces when I drop her, rolling straight over and lifting her ass up to wriggle her damp underwear down her thighs. I yank them straight off her, and the memory of stuffing her mouth with them a few years ago shudders through me. She loved it, but tonight I want to hear her when I make her scream.

Behind her, I strip out of my clothes but leave the ski mask on. My skin prickles with sweat, a mix of summer heat and feral energy pouring off of me.

"Do I need a condom when I fuck your whore cunt?" I ask her, grabbing her delicious, round ass roughly, then bringing my hand down for a firm smack. My words are harsh, but the unspoken question hangs between us. When she shakes her head, I know in my heart she's telling me she hasn't been with anyone since me.

"Good girl," I tell her, bending to kiss away the sting. "Get that ass up and spread yourself open."

"Oh fuck, yes," she moans, reaching back to follow my orders.

"Is that what you want, baby? Want me to use these holes and fill them up and make them mine?" I spit onto the tight muscle there, and the sight of it dripping down and mixing with her slickness makes my cock throb even harder. "Too late, sweetheart. They're already fucking mine."

I hitch her higher and line my cock up with her aching pussy. The way she's got me feeling, I could come right now, but I need this to be so good for her.

"Look at me, Kayla. Look me in the eye so I can see them widen when I fill you."

She twists her shoulders to look back up at me. I must look fucking insane in nothing but a black mask, but from the way she bites her lip, I know she loves it.

The urge to plunge straight in is strong, but I go slowly instead, forcing her to feel every inch as I claim her. When my hips meet the curve of her ass, I'm all the way in, and I need to take a moment to breathe and cherish it. I caress my hand down the length of her spine, admiring her strong back muscles, her full hips, and toned thighs.

"You good, baby?" I ask, softly.

"Ruin me," she begs, reaching one arm behind her back. I cup her tattoo to pin her in place, then slide my cock out and let loose.

Wet, filthy sounds fill the room, harsh breaths and deep groans rolling out of me with every thrust. I fuck her hard and fast. Deeper and deeper. Kayla doesn't talk much, leaning into her submissive role, but her moans are loud, guttural, and cut off with *'yes'*. *'Fuck'*. *'More'*.

She feels incredible, and though I'd love it to last longer, I know we have all week to take advantage of each other. When I'm not sure I can hold off much longer, I flip her over and thrust straight back in, moving one hand to her clit and yanking the mask off with the other.

"Get there now, baby. Come on my cock."

She grabs at her breasts, hips bucking up to meet my every thrust, and I watch my girl throw her head back at the exact moment she tightens around me and lets her orgasm take over. I grab her thighs and pull her tight onto me, holding her in place while my cock explodes, jet after jet pulsing into her warm pussy.

"Holy fuck," she pants, beautiful and glowing. She stares up at me and swallows hard. "What... the fuck... was that?"

Chapter 42
Ryan

After I clean her up, Kayla lies sideways across the bed, staring up at me with her head on my stomach. With my eyes closed, I stroke one hand through her hair, and let the fingers on my other hand weave in and out of hers. I can't imagine life in any other world would be better than this.

"Ryan?" she whispers.

"Yeah, baby?"

"What's wrong with us?"

My eyes snap open. "What do you mean?"

"I mean that was the hottest thing we've ever done and what does it mean when I get off on you breaking into my bedroom, and you get off on me telling you shit I've done with other guys."

I sit back against the headboard and pull her up until she's laying in my arms, her cheek pressed to my chest.

"There's nothing wrong with us, Kayla. We're just two filthy freaks who shouldn't be living on opposite sides of the world. What are you feeling?"

"Shame, I guess."

"You don't need to feel ashamed or guilty or embarrassed or anything negative at all, babe. Everything you like is good, and I'm into it too. I'd tell you if I wasn't, and you know you can change your mind any time."

I lose track of time staring at her, stroking her loose strands of hair away from her face.

"We're not like other couples," I tell her. "I've never been like this with other people."

"No, I'm not either," she sighs.

"Well, I'm honoured to be the man who gets to see all the sides of you. The inside, the outside. The backside." I reach down and give it a playful smack, hoping it doesn't hurt after the rougher ones from earlier. "Especially fond of that side."

"You came early," she whispers, stroking my face as if she's checking I'm really here.

"Yeah, well, once you've travelled halfway across the world to see someone, it seemed stupid to stop only three hours away."

She hums softly and flutters her eyes closed. I wrap my arms a little tighter and pull the blankets up over us. It's a warm night, but I've always loved being cocooned with her.

"It was like my body knew you were closer than usual. I couldn't concentrate, couldn't sit still. Couldn't eat or think about anything except how much I wanted to be here with you."

"That's almost romantic," she laughs.

"Hey, I can be romantic."

"Sure, I'll believe it when I see it."

"Oh, you'll believe it. You're getting non-stop, 24/7 romance for the rest of this trip. Starting now."

"I don't know if I can have sex again yet," she winces. "That was fucking intense."

"I was not talking about sex. That's on you, dirty girl." I press a kiss to her forehead and peel back the covers. "Go open the front part of my backpack."

She climbs off of me and pads across the floor, bending to unzip my bag. Inside I've stashed three packs of Red Vines, the candy she got immediately hooked on when she came to visit.

"Oh my God," she squeals, clutching them to her chest. "I love you so much."

Her back snaps up straight, eyes widening as they lock with mine. We've never said those words before, and to hear it tumble out, raw and unfiltered, is fucking incredible.

"You're welcome."

I'm dying to say it back, but not like this. I will soon though, and I know the perfect spot for a declaration.

Chapter 43
Kayla

WHILE I STRETCH OUT like a cat after the best sleep of my life, Ryan's voice flows through the chalet, singing away in the shower. I can't tell if it's some country song or if he's putting on an accent, but all I know is he's here.

He's here.

His arrival last night was a complete surprise. My body went into shock when he grabbed me in my room, but as soon as I heard his voice, I knew I was safe. Ryan played his role well, and I leaned into the fantasy and took everything he had to give. The tender ache between my thighs is a reminder of that.

Falling asleep in his arms afterwards would have been all the comfort I needed to recover from the adrenaline rush, but he went even further with a warm shower followed by a candlelit massage that was so good I cried happy tears.

I expect him to crawl back into bed with me, but he heads downstairs, and the singing continues with a backdrop of clattering pans and cupboard doors opening and closing. Eventually, curiosity gets the better of me. I pull on one of his t-shirts and pad downstairs to the main part of the chalet.

In the kitchen, I find him wearing nothing but tight black boxer briefs, and a Christmas apron he must have found in the cupboard. He cracks eggs into little ramekins, and tops them with cream from the fridge and lots of fresh black pepper. Next to punnets of fresh berries and yoghurt, warm baguettes are waiting to be torn open and slathered with jam.

I'm only staying in the house for a couple of weeks while my parents have an electric carport installed, so I haven't bothered stocking up on groceries. He must have snuck out early to go to the shops down the hill.

"What's going on here?"

His smile is miles wide when he looks sideways to find me standing in the doorway in his t-shirt. He makes no effort to pretend he's not checking out my legs as his gaze dips lower and lower.

"Breakfast, Bunny. I hope you're hungry."

"Ravenous," I tell him, coming up behind him, and admiring the view of his firm ass and strong thighs. I stroke my fingertips down the length of his spine, and when he ignores me, I run my tongue all the way back up, giving his glutes a firm squeeze.

When he removes my hands, I reach up and rake my nails through the strands of hair at the back of his neck instead. He shivers, and tries to swat me away, so I go for gold and slip my hand inside his apron, and down the front of his underwear. He's already hard, like I hoped he might be. If I had a dick, it would never go down when he's around.

His focus remains on grating a wedge of local hard cheese on top of the eggs, but I want all of his attention, and I want it now. At his side, I drop to my knees and shuffle between him and the under-counter cupboards. There's not a lot of room, but it's no hardship to press my face against him, to reach underneath his apron and cup him firmly.

"Enough!" he squeals, hoisting me up to sit on the counter and pointing a playful finger in my face. "Stop distracting me."

"Why won't you let me touch you?"

"I don't think it's very romantic to let your girlfriend blow you on the kitchen floor before you've made sure she's well fed."

My stomach drops like we're flying over the lip of a vertical drop rollercoaster. He might have turned me brainless from all the orgasms, but I don't remember any conversation about putting labels on this thing.

"Are we playing house now?" I slither off the counter to fill a glass of water.

"We sure are," he says, returning to his cooking. "I told you last night, for as long as I'm here, you're getting the full Ryan Richmond boyfriend experience."

"Oh, because you have so much experience."

I'm teasing, but how would I know? All those years we didn't talk about our lives outside of winters. He might have had a hundred girlfriends.

"Sweetheart, I have a lifetime of experience with you."

He always knows how to get me out of my head, but sometimes he says these things that send me deep inside it. I drink my water while staring out of the kitchen window at the quiet street below us. I took some of my first steps on that street, made snowmen with my dad, held my grandmother's hand so she wouldn't slip on icy patches.

Sometimes I long for those simple days, before jobs and worries and boys. Who would have thought the little girl back then would be here now with the boy from up the hill?

Ryan slips the tray of ramekins into the oven, washes his hands, and comes closer. His arms wrap around my waist, and he holds me close to his chest, kissing his way from my temple to my jaw.

He spins me to face him and when our foreheads touch, it's as if he's staring into my soul. When it gets too intense, I try to look away, but he tips my chin up and takes his time looking at me, eyes roaming everywhere. The corners of his mouth keep curling at whatever memory he's thinking of.

"Now," he says, kissing the end of my nose. "Eggs *en cocotte* take twelve minutes to cook. So..."

He unties his apron and hangs it back up with a slow ease that has my heart rate kicking up a gear. His voice dips to a sexy drawl he knows drives me wild. "It may not be very romantic to accept a blow job, but that rule doesn't work both ways."

His fingers trace up the inside of my thigh, dancing around where the line of my underwear would sit if I'd worn any.

"Are you sore?"

"A little," I confess and he kneels before me.

"Let me see if I can kiss it better."

Chapter 44
Kayla

I'VE KEPT WORK TO a minimum this week, but when I do have to work, Ryan meets me at the base station afterwards, with a bouquet of wildflowers he's picked himself. July boasts beautiful days, so we walk down the mountain hand in hand, and plan out our next day.

At home, we take cold beers to the hot tub, then shower together before heading out to dinner. Whether it's pizza in the village while the sun goes down, or one of the more upmarket restaurants in town, these are the best meals of my life.

In the mornings he cooks breakfast, or we wake up with our hands and mouths all over each other before we've even opened our eyes.

I could get used to this. I *am* getting used to this, and that's a big problem. Pretending is easy when he looks at me like I've hung the moon, says all the right things, and acts like this is forever. Except it's not forever, and with every hour the clock counts down, the knot in my stomach gets bigger and bigger.

On my days off, we pack a bag and head out early to one of our favourite spots. We start our journey the same way we would in winter, by riding the *Telecabin* most of the way up the mountain. From there, the chairlift takes you closer to the summit, but we prefer to hike up and take a ride back down.

Today we're heading for the highest point on our side of the valley, the same spot where we go in winter, then race to the bottom. Whenever I bring clients here, I hang back while they take their photos. The view isn't nearly as stunning without him to share it with.

Our path drifts through thick forests and alpine meadows. In the winter months, snow covers all of this, but now herds of cows and goats roam freely. Apart from the occasional cowbell and the call of black grouse, there is mostly silence. I've never known peace like it.

At just under 6000 ft, the peak boasts panoramic views for miles, hills and forests in every shade of green. In the far distance, Mont Blanc shines down on us all, the top still covered in snow and ice even in July.

Once we find a comfy spot, we spread out a picnic blanket and dig our lunches out of our backpacks. There's barely a cloud in the sky, so I top up my sunscreen while Ryan sprawls out on the grass beside me.

"Hot tub will feel so good later. My legs are killing me."

I almost tell him he'd get used to it if he lived here, we could come here all the time. That this spot only makes me happy if he's here to share it with.

Being here with him in winter always makes me contemplative, but in summer my mood is more sombre.

"Will you keep your chalet after your parents die?" I ask him, and he chokes on his electrolyte drink.

"Bit dark, Bunny. Are your parents OK?"

"They're fine. I'm just wondering what the future holds, I guess."

"I'd never really thought about it. I imagine it'll go to me and Hannah, and unless it's a money pit, I can't see why we wouldn't keep it. What about you? Would you sell your chalet?"

"Never," I tell him. "I'd keep hold of it for as long as I could. My dad loved holidays here when he was a kid. My grandmother would hate to see it sold. She wanted me to keep coming for as long as possible, to bring my own kids someday. Teach them to ski the same slopes she did."

Ryan scoots closer and puts his arm around my shoulder. "Is that what you want?"

Yes. No. Maybe. How am I supposed to know?

"Do you ever wish we'd met under different circumstances?" I ask. I don't know why I'm entertaining these thoughts, but they keep getting the better of me.

"What do you mean?"

"Like if we met in a bar or something. If you'd asked me out, and we went to dinner, made out on a doorstep somewhere. If we didn't have so much complicated history?"

He takes a bite of his sandwich and chews slowly, like it pains him to get through it.

"I don't think so. No."

"No? What if we'd met at university somewhere? We might have hated each other. Or maybe we would..."

I can't finish the sentence, it gets stuck behind the lump in my throat. Ryan sets his lunchbox down and pulls me into his lap. I go easily though I know it's a bad idea. This is my fault for getting deep and meaningful. I should have kept it light and safe. Talked about the clouds, even though there are none.

"Look at me," he says, cupping my face between his hands. "Do I wish our circumstances were different now? Sure, absolutely I do. But I wouldn't swap the lifetime of memories we've made for anything. And we have a lot more to make."

Tears threaten to spill when I sense what's coming, and I shake my head to get rid of them. "No."

"Yes, Kayla," he smiles. "Nobody else is ever coming close to you. I love you. You're it. North star."

My eyes prick with tears, and a memory from last night pushes to the forefront. "You're only saying that because I said—"

"Nope," he says, cutting me off with a kiss. "I'm saying it because I love you, and now I have said it, I don't know why I've waited so long."

He tips his head back and yells at the big, blue sky above us.

"I love Kayla McInnes!"

He presses his hand to his heart, and instinctively, I do the same. Except while he's celebrating, I'm trying my best to hold mine in.

Chapter 45
Kayla
Thirteen Winters Ago / Age Fifteen

RYAN PULLS DOWN THE safety bar on the last chairlift of the day. This year we're trying to catch the last lift to the top of the mountain every day, then ski all the way back down for steaming mugs of *chocolat chaud* and salty *frites*.

"*Vite, vite!*" the lift-operators call out every time, hurrying us when we barrel through the gates as they're trying to close. I know we'll miss it eventually, but for now it's a rush every time. That's us, two adrenaline junkies. We're always chasing the next thrill and have been since we were old enough to ski.

"Can I ask you a question?" he says, coughing to clear his throat.

I angle my body towards him. "Of course, always."

He sucks in a deep breath and blurts out his question. "Have you ever kissed anyone?"

His expression is hidden behind his goggles, and I'm glad he can't see mine because my eyes are wide and full of panic. I was not expecting him to ask me that.

We almost never talk about our lives back home on these trips to the mountains. They've always been our chance to escape to a place full of magic and wonder, but Ryan has been quieter than usual all afternoon. I wonder how long he's been waiting to ask me.

"Yeah, I have." I wish it wasn't my answer, but I'd never lie to him.

"Oh."

Oh? Who says 'oh'? Does he not think I'm kissable?

"That surprises you?"

"Yeah. No, I mean, I was only asking. What was it like?"

"It was awful." I give him the briefest of details. I'm sure Ryan doesn't really care to know he bumped my teeth with his, shoved his tongue in my mouth, then bolted before I had the chance to kiss him back.

Opportunities for kissing boys are slim when you go to an all girl's school, but at Sophie Mulligan's birthday, her brother invited some friends, and I saw my chance and took it. I don't exactly regret it, but I don't think it should count as a first kiss at all, actually. It was brief, horrid, and revoltingly wet. I didn't even know his name.

I'd hoped for a fairytale movie star kiss. Doesn't every girl deserve that? If not for her first kiss, then at least once in her life. I want to be kissed so hard it makes my toes curl, by someone who knows what they're doing, and who makes me feel like the prettiest girl in the world.

I want to be kissed by Ryan.

"Why do you ask?"

He looks down and knocks the tips of his skis together. "No reason."

Yeah right. He's a terrible liar.

"Have *you* ever kissed someone?"

"Not yet," he mumbles.

The chairlift carries us out of the wind and for a moment there is perfect silence. Ryan tips his head back and groans. A perfect cloud of hot breath fills the cold air above him. I want to reach out and grab it and shove it in my mouth.

"You know what, though? I've never kissed someone at the top of a mountain. You want to be *that* first?"

"Sure." He shrugs like it's no big deal, but the pink in his cheeks stays for the rest of the trip.

Chapter 46
Ryan

Of course our happiness can't last.

Kayla is gone when I wake up the next morning, and I find her sitting on the floor at the far end of the first-floor balcony, her knees pulled to her chest. I drop into the space next to her and quickly learn there isn't enough room for us both between the wall and the outdoor armchair.

"You're squishing me," she says, shoving me away. I shift round to sit facing her instead, trapping her knees between mine.

"I'm sorry. I want to soak up every minute."

"You only need to do that because you know you're leaving, so every minute feels like it's slipping away. It hurts."

What hurts is us doing this dance again. I'm so fucking over it. Living apart sucks, but this week has been incredible, and it's only proved to me how much we are supposed to be together.

I don't know how we make it happen, but I know we're not going back to being just friends, and I won't let her push me away again.

"I can't lose you," I whisper, cupping the backs of her calves and smoothing my thumbs up and down her soft skin.

"I'm not yours to lose."

"Well, I'm yours, Bunny."

Kayla finally looks at me, her head tipped to one side. She pulls her lips behind her teeth and shakes her head ever so slowly.

"Why won't you give us a chance?" I ask.

"Because I don't know how to be in your life if it's not in the mountains. I thought we might be something more, but we're only good for skiing and fucking."

How can she possibly think that's true when we've spent our week talking, sharing meals, and relaxing together? We've felt like an old couple on vacation taking some time to reconnect, not friends who won't admit their feelings for each other.

"Kayla, come on. You mean so much more to me than that."

"Then how is it so easy for you to leave?"

"You think it's easy?" I snap. "I already know I'm going to feel like shit the second we say goodbye. I'll be counting down the minutes until I can call you, and the days until next winter."

Reaching up to grip the railing, she pulls herself up to standing. I get up too, and when she tries to push past me, I reach both arms out wide to block her path.

"You're pulling away. Please don't ruin our last few hours together."

"Oh, I'm the one ruining it? You're the one who ruined our deal with all of this," she shouts, throwing her arms out wide. "It's too much, Ryan!"

"What is?"

"All of it. The sweet gestures and the fake words and your goddamn postcards. You need to stop sending them. They destroy me."

There must be over twenty now, including the one I wrote while she was sleeping next to me in California. Writing them has become something of a weekly ritual. Grabbing a coffee and a postcard from one of the tourist shops on my way to work, then writing my notes to her while I eat lunch.

To learn they make her feel this way is agony.

"OK fine, I'll stop sending them," I agree, not wanting this sadness to taint any more of our time. "C'mere."

She steps into my open arms and lets me hold her like that for a while, her hands on my hips, mine rubbing her back.

"What is this really about?"

"What the fuck am I supposed to do when you go back home and I have to remember this was all a game?"

"You're not a game."

"This has always been a game!" she yells, pulling away and ducking underneath my arm. "*'See you next winter, fuck buddy.'* That's what we are."

Rushing after her, I try to catch her arm, but she whips it away. This can't be happening. This can't really be what she thinks of us.

"Bullshit. Bullshit. You have never been a game to me, and you're lying to yourself if you think that's all this is. I love you, Kayla."

A desperate sensation locks in my chest.

"I can't keep falling for you over and over," she says, slumping onto the sofa, sobbing into her hands. "It gets worse every winter. And stop telling me you love me. It's cruel at this point."

I shove her parents' coffee table aside and kneel in front of her.

"Kayla, look at me," I plead. "I can't stop loving you. It's not possible."

She sniffs, her shoulders shaking as she tries to keep it under control. I stroke my hands up and down her arms, wishing I knew how to comfort her.

"I couldn't tell you the exact moment I fell in love with you because every year I fall even harder. I didn't come here for the mountains, I came here for you. How many times do I have to tell you before you believe me?"

"I can't, Ryan. I can't believe it, only to watch you take it away."

"I don't want to go," I tell her. "You must know that? This is killing me."

"But you can't stay," she shrugs. She looks defeated and exhausted. It makes me wonder if she's gotten any sleep at all. "Can you?"

"We can make it work."

"What if we can't?"

"What if we *can*? I believe in us. You're the one thing I know is true." It breaks my heart to see her cry, knowing I'm trying my hardest to fix things. "This is not it for us, Kayla."

"I can't do it," she says, pushing past me to head for the stairs.

"I'll do anything. There's no mountain I won't climb," I call after her.

"You're *literally* leaving in two hours."

"I know, and I fucking hate it. It might take me a little while to figure everything out, but I promise you, we'll be together in this world. I'll make sure of it."

With her bedroom door closed, I don't know if she hears me, but it doesn't matter. I know it's true.

Chapter 47
Kayla
Fifteen Winters Ago / Age Thirteen

This is the worst Christmas ever. Everything sucks, I hate it here, and I want to go home.

"What are you reading?" Ryan asks, flopping onto the sofa next to me. He is careful not to knock my leg, which is propped up on a pile of cushions, my ankle in an inflatable cast until we go home to Scotland.

"It's about quantum theory. Someone left it on the bookshelf." I've already read everything else in the house, including the ones that are definitely too grown up for me. If I'd known I was going to spend this winter sitting on the sofa, I would have brought a suitcase full of books from home.

"Boring," he says, unwrapping the shiny foil from another gold chocolate coin.

"It's not, actually. It's this idea that there are many worlds, and in those worlds there are other versions of us, living totally different lives."

"That's creepy. What if one of the other versions of me is a serial killer or something?"

Trust Ryan to think of something so stupid right when I was feeling hopeful for the first time since my accident.

"It means there's a world where I didn't hurt my leg," I tell him, lifting the book higher and hoping he'll shut up. He has chocolate on his cheek, but I don't tell him.

"Does it mean there's a world where you're a bunny, Bunny?"

"You could be skiing right now."

Just because I can't do anything, doesn't mean he has to stay home with me all day. I'm perfectly capable of staying here on my own, but he's insisted, and that's annoyed me even more.

"I told you, if you can't ski, then I won't either. I got you something to cheer you up, though."

I was expecting more chocolate, since he's brought some every day, but he digs in his pocket and hands me a small black box instead.

"What's this?" I ask. We don't normally get each other Christmas presents.

"Open it and see."

I snap open the lid and find a silver necklace with a pretty snowflake pendant inside.

"Why did you do this?"

"Mum and I picked it out yesterday. So you'll always have a piece of snow with you, even when it's not winter."

Chapter 48
Ryan

My flight home connects via Paris, but the pain I felt on that first short flight gave me all the clarity I needed.

Kayla is right, as usual. Telling her she means the world to me doesn't mean shit if I'm following it up with a tearful goodbye.

She was quiet for most of the drive and dropped me off outside the airport without even saying *'see you next winter'*. She's protecting herself, I get it, but I never want my last memory to be of her turning away from me.

While waiting to board my connecting flight, I call the one person who can always figure things out in a crisis.

"Oh, finally he deigns to grace us with a phone call," Dad says. "What happened to our dinner last week?"

"Yeah, sorry about that," I wince. "I flew out early to see Kayla. Couldn't wait."

"That's alright, son, Hannah told me. Kayla doing OK?"

"Yeah, she's great. Listen, I don't have long because I'm about to board my flight back to L.A., but I'm calling because I need a job. In London. As soon as possible."

"Well, you're a degree or two short for anything I could offer you, I'm afraid," he laughs.

"Not a law job, obviously, but anything in television or film. I'll reach out to contacts on the flight home, but can you please do me a favour and do the same? Literally *anything*, Dad. I'm desperate."

"Of course, son. I'll put some feelers out," he says, his voice growing concerned. "What's going on? Are you in trouble?"

"I'm coming home."

Home means nothing, if Kayla isn't part of it. I might not be able to move my work to the mountains, but I'll move it as close as possible if it means more time with her.

Word spreads fast, and by the time I'm in my seat, Cameron has emailed me a link to check out.

Subject: Job idea?

Chapter 49
Kayla

By late September, the summer vacation crowds have gone, though car rallies and mountain bike races still bring people to the area on weekends. Hiking tours will slow down until the snow comes again in late November, which gives me a couple of months to unwind after a busy summer, and start preparing for next winter.

There's barely been a moment to stop and reflect on how far I've come this year, certainly not while my head and my heart have spent most of it obsessing over Ryan.

My calendar is already two-thirds full for winter, with off-piste ski touring, some family lessons, and a couple of weekends volunteering as a marshal for a freestyle ski and snowboard tournament. A few friends from Edinburgh have booked flights to come and crash with me for long weekends, too.

There's so much to look forward to, I'm not even worried about whether Ryan comes home this winter. We've exchanged a few texts since he flew home in July, but things aren't the same anymore. I haven't asked about this December, and he hasn't mentioned it. Turns out being friends with benefits isn't sustainable long term, and honestly, it would probably be for the best if he didn't come.

We gave it our best shot, with the time we could spare for each other, and it didn't work out. There's no shame in that, but there's also no point wasting another year of my life on the impossible. A winter without him would give me a proper chance to move on and think about what I really want from this next decade of my life.

Soon the mountain resorts will be full of the next generation of energetic, young seasonnaires, ready to make new friendships and memories. The memories typically last longer than the friendships, thanks to the transient nature of the work.

Nothing is ever really permanent around here, and part of me wonders what it would be like to have that kind of reliability in my life.

I'm almost thirty. I can't be crawling bars and running pickup games forever. The guys who move here long term usually bring a girlfriend, a dog, and a campervan with them.

I don't even know why I'm thinking about men. I don't need them. Not a single one of them, especially with a box of toys underneath my bed, and a stack of romance novels to make up for their failings.

Love wasn't what brought me here, anyway. I moved here for me, because the mountains have always been the place I felt happiest, because the first run of the day will wake you up quicker than any cup of coffee. I moved here because even on cold dark days where the snowfall is so thick you can't see the other side of the slope, I feel like I'm part of something bigger. Something special.

No two days are alike, and getting to see the mountain in her ever-changing glory is a gift. Every ascent and descent has something new to admire. Every client brings their own stories and experiences, and all of them make my life even richer.

The biggest benefit of living here year round is getting to enjoy the full four seasons of food on offer. In summer I eat a lot of fish and grains, but these cooler days have me craving something rich and hearty, a dish I can make and enjoy over a few evenings on the sofa with a good book.

There's a bigger supermarket twenty minutes drive down the mountain, but I like to get what I can from our local greengrocer, butcher, and bakery. I choose fresh *girolles* and *cèpes* mushrooms, the first of the season, a bag of risotto rice, and a bulb of garlic the size of my fist. Early squash will make an excellent soup if I roast them with olive oil and thyme, and I need nothing more than plump, ripe pears to sink my teeth into for pudding.

On my way out, I run straight into a customer on his way in, bouncing off the wall of his chest.

"*Je suis désolé,*" I say, rubbing at the spot on my forehead that I hope won't bruise. An injured ski guide is not a good look. Two hands grip my shoulders, steadying me in the doorway.

"Sorry, Bunny, I didn't see you there."

My head snaps up, and I swear I must be hallucinating, but no. Ryan Richmond is here, in all his gorgeous glory.

"What are you doing?"

"Me? Grabbing some supplies for dinner," he says, holding up a bag from the butcher's next door.

How hard did I hit my head?

"Not here in the supermarket," I hiss. "*Here,* here. What are you doing in town?"

"Oh," he shrugs, a subtle smirk creeping up at the corner of his mouth. "I live here now."

An embarrassing noise catches in the back of my throat, tears pricking up out of nowhere.

"What do you mean, you live here now?"

"*Je vis ici maintenant.*"

"What the fuck?" I punch him in the arm, and honestly, he deserves it. "Stop being so obtuse with me. Since when?"

"I've been here..." he counts off the fingers on one hand, grinning as he stalls me. "Five days, I think. Still a little jetlagged."

"*Why* are you here?"

Ryan cocks his head to one side and takes a deep breath.

His mouth opens and closes a couple of times, and whatever he's struggling to say, I wish he'd hurry up and spit it out.

"I left something precious behind, and I needed to come back for it."

His bottom lip wobbles for a second before he bites down on it. I don't know whether to kiss him or burst into tears, so instead we stand there staring at years of history, a cocktail of emotions fighting their way to the front. Ryan blinks first, rolling his eyes the way he always has when I beat him at something.

"I win," I whisper, mostly to myself. His hand comes up between us, one fingertip poised to tap the tip of my nose, but he pulls away and shoves his hand deep in the pocket of his jeans.

"It was good to run into you, Kayla," he says, stepping around me.

"Where are you going?"

"To get the rest of my groceries, then home to make dinner. Chicken and leek pie. Would you like to join me?"

"For dinner?"

"Yes, for dinner," he says softly, and I don't understand any of what's happening right now.

Why isn't he inviting me over for hot tub sex? Why isn't he dragging me there right now, one hand up inside my shirt? Why is he here at all?

"I have plans," I tell him, leaving out the part where those plans are stirring a pan of risotto for an hour while I drink the rest of the bottle of white wine and watch back-to-back episodes of Gilmore Girls.

"Maybe some other time, then. I'll see you around."

When he grabs a basket, he spins to face me, that boyish smile spread right across his face. "You look great, by the way," he calls out, leaving me blushing in the doorway, wondering what alternative reality I've slipped into.

Seeing him takes me right back to those summer nights we spent together two months ago. The closeness, companionship, and acceptance. Days where I had someone to hug me at the end of a long bike tour, someone who shared the mental load and took care of me.

Someone who knows the real me, not just fun mountain Kayla, who's always got her game face on and up for an adventure. The Kayla who he loves, and who loves him back.

Chapter 50
Ryan

It kills me to be this close to Kayla and not run straight into her arms, but something she said in the summer has been playing on my mind.

We've never had a chance to date or get to know each other outside of winters, and I want to give her that experience. Want to prove to her we're so much more than festive friends-with-benefits. In my heart, I know she's the one, but if this plan is going to work, I need to let things happen at her pace.

Unfortunately, my girl is stubborn and competitive. She probably knows I'm up to something and is determined to win, even if she doesn't know what game we're playing.

Sitting at home waiting for Kayla to knock on my door every night quickly gets boring, and if I wanted to spend every waking hour attached to my computer, I would have stayed in California. So I do the same thing everyone does when they're new in town. I pick up a bar job.

We've been coming to Rico's since we were old enough to pass for the legal drinking age, but seeing it from the other side of the bar is something else. Nights aren't as busy as they will be once the snow arrives, but the music and cheap drinks still draw people in.

It only takes a couple of weeks to figure out who's here long term and who's passing through. Familiar faces become friends, and a few guys invite me to go mountain-biking with them sometime.

That I don't own a mountain bike doesn't seem to be a problem. Someone's always got a spare to lend a friend.

It takes longer than expected for Kayla to come in, which has left me wondering how she spends her evenings, and with who. I hear her first, her warm laugh pouring out of her when she strolls in with a group of friends.

She looks hot as fuck in a short skirt and ankle boots, her tight white t-shirt accentuating her curves. Her hair flows over her shoulders in loose curls, and there's a slick of pink lipstick painted across her pretty mouth. If I wasn't already head over heels for her, I'd be falling right now.

The other women are dressed similarly, a group keen to start their night with a bang, not one desperate for refreshment after a day of hiking. Kayla doesn't notice me as she leads her friends to the table across from the bar, and only stops laughing when she glances up and catches me staring at her. She hops off her stool and eats up the space between us in seconds.

"What are you doing?"

"Serving drinks. What can I get for you, miss?"

"You work here?"

I pluck at the white Rico's logo on my black t-shirt, the same one all the staff are required to wear. "Sure looks that way."

"Why the fuck are you working in Rico's bar, Ryan? Why are you living here and wandering around the town like you belong here?"

"What can I say? I'm living the dream."

"Hollywood is your dream," she spits out, and I'm not sure I've ever seen her this pissed off.

I lean across the bar and stroke a line from between her eyebrows to the tip of her nose. "You are my dream, Kayla. Since forever. Now, did you want something to drink, or can I serve someone else?"

She storms off without ordering, and I bite back a smile. I'm not trying to make her angry, but I'm not here to put any pressure on her, either. I know in my heart this is the right move.

She can ignore me all she wants, but I've always known we'd be endgame if only we lived in the same place. Well, now we do, and I'm prepared to put in the work and show her how serious I am, no matter how long it takes. I've waited a lifetime, I can be patient.

Even on quiet nights, there's plenty to do behind the bar, and from the corner of my eye I see her friends laughing and joking while she does her best to stay in a bad mood. A short brunette ignores Kayla's attempts to yank her back to the table and saunters over.

I've never met this woman before, but she looks like a lot of fun. "Welcome to Rico's. What can I get for you?"

"Five pale ales, please."

"Coming right up." I get to work pulling their drinks and try not to laugh at the way she keeps looking back at their table.

"Are you sitting with my friend Kayla over there?" I ask.

"Yeah. You see that tall blonde in the middle," she says, pointing over her shoulder with her thumb. "She and I are getting married next month. We went to school with Kayla and this is our big send-off."

"Ah, then these are on me." I nod my head in their direction. "Congrats to you and your lady."

She bursts out laughing. "Kayla said you'd try to give us free drinks, and I'm not supposed to take them."

"Oh, did she now?" I smile, then lean across the bar and lower my voice. "Maybe this can be our little secret?"

She winks at me. "You're Ryan, right?"

"In the flesh."

"I'm Allie," she says, offering me her hand. While we shake, she squeezes hard and doesn't hide the fact she's giving me the once over. "Fuck, I get it now."

"Get what?"

"Why she waited for you."

"What do you mean?"

She just laughs and nudges three beers into a triangle so she can carry them to her table.

"Let me give you a hand."

"You'd better stay put if you want to make it through the night. I'll come back in a second."

Chapter 51
Ryan

No matter how hot it's been to talk about being with other people in the past, watching a string of guys hit on Kayla and her friends is fucking horrible. I don't like it one bit, but they can handle their own, and waste no time making it clear they're only interested in each other's company tonight.

Her friends take turns to visit me at the bar, first for beers, then for shots, and soon I've met Allie's fiancée Mel, as well as their other friends Katie and Anna. Kayla keeps her back to me the whole time, and I'm impressed with her stubbornness, but also want to have a little fun. When the bar is quiet, I head over to collect their empty glasses.

I tap her on the shoulder and clear my throat. "Excuse me, miss?"

"What?" she sulks, and I take a deep breath and roll my shoulders back.

"Uh, my name is Ryan, and I couldn't help but notice you from my spot behind the bar over there. I was wondering, would you like to go out with me sometime?"

She blinks at me like I've asked her to jump off a chairlift. "What are you doing?"

"Shooting my shot," I beam. "What do you say?"

"Are you asking me on a date?"

"Yes, I am. Can I take you out for dinner and drinks, hold your hand while I walk you home and, if I'm ever so lucky, maybe give you a goodnight kiss?"

The collective gasp from her friends has me hiding my smile behind my fist.

"No," Kayla says, twisting her barstool away from me.

"No?" her friends shriek in unison. God, I love these people. I duck around her to ask again.

"I think we could have a really nice life together," I tell her, then cough obnoxiously. "Did I say life? I meant night, sorry."

"Do it! Do it!" her friends chant, banging the table until her face breaks into a smile.

"No seeing me in the dark." She prods me in the sternum, but I grab her hand and hold it there. "You're too tempting. It's dangerous."

The idea that we're only drawn to each other in nocturnal hours is hilarious. I don't think there's an hour of the day we haven't fooled around one way or another.

"Breakfast then."

"Deal," she says quickly, slapping her hand over her mouth as if that will take it back.

"Tomorrow?"

"Not unless you want this lot to join us," she says.

"Are you all staying with Kayla?"

"No," Katie tells me. "We're in the three-bed rental."

"Nice. And is she staying with you, or will someone help her get home?"

"We think you should help her get home," one of the other friends says.

"No problem," I say at the same time Kayla speaks.

"Absolutely not. No. Not allowed to take me home. No way."

"OK ladies. If there's one thing I know about Miss McInnes here, it's that we don't argue with her, ever. What Kayla wants, Kayla gets, but I'm gonna need some reassurance from one of you that you'll text me and tell me she got home safe. Deal?"

All four of them shove their phones in my direction and I make a big scene about saving my number in all of them, telling them I hope they keep in touch. Kayla does her best impression of a scowl, and before I get back to work, I tap the little snowflake dangling at the hollow of her throat and give her a wink.

"Cute necklace, Bunny."

Chapter 52

Ryan

Eighteen Winters Ago / Age Ten

Last year, our parents promised we could go to the very top of the mountain when we turned ten, and today is the day. Dad takes a million photos, but I want to get going.

"Race you to the bottom, Bunny."

"Why do you keep calling me Bunny?"

"Because your braids look like rabbit ears when you wear them like that. And your nose wrinkles when you laugh."

"Does not."

"It does." I tap her on the tip of her nose. It's cold and pink. "Boop! You're a bunny with two bunny ears and a little bunny nose."

"I don't think you've ever seen a real rabbit," she says, sliding past me. "Last one down is a rotten egg!"

Chapter 53
Kayla

For what is, apparently, our second date, Ryan invites me over for dinner at his parent's chalet. Whatever the fuck that's supposed to mean.

Any other time we've been alone in this house, we've headed straight for his bedroom and stripped as fast as possible. It feels awkward to be here for any other purpose, but what does it say I'm more comfortable around him with my clothes off than on?

Nobody's lighting fires this early, and without Cheryl's beautiful tree in the corner, and sparkling decorations hanging from the mantlepiece, the house feels bare. It's like I've slipped into some dream state, a familiar location with an unfamiliar mindset.

"You can sit," he tells me, but sitting down feels far too formal. This isn't right. I'm not supposed to be here. *He's* not supposed to be here. The plan was to live my best life without giving him a second thought.

Instead, he's everywhere.

In all the shops, working in my favourite bar, in my friend's text messages after swapping numbers to make sure I got home after Allie and Mel's pre-wedding celebrations.

Mel told me they've invited him, a man they met for three hours in a bar, to their wedding. It's ridiculous. There's no way I'm letting that happen, and I already RSVP'd without a plus one.

A few days ago, he called to invite me on our first date, something I apparently agreed to after several shots of tequila. I only agreed because I was hungry, but then he picked me up wearing a henley and a backwards cap, and I was done for. We walked three streets to a little cafe that does the best omelettes in town and made the awkward small talk people make on first dates.

Food, weather, music, movies. All stuff I already know about him, some silly game of roleplay that fucked with my head so badly I couldn't concentrate for the rest of the day. After he paid for our food, he walked me home and told me he had to get work, but that he hoped our second date would last longer.

So here I am, pacing the length of his living room, wondering what prompted him to abandon his dreams and flip his life upside down.

"How long are you planning to stay here?" I ask when he hands me a chilled glass of Sancerre.

"Forever, hopefully. You look beautiful, by the way."

Ordinarily I wouldn't give my clothes more than a second thought, so God knows why I emptied my entire wardrobe out before settling on a blue sundress with tiny white flowers and a cute knitted cardigan. It's not very me, and neither are the meticulous curls I've styled in my hair. Stupid boy has gotten me acting insane.

I clink my glass against his. "You'll live in this house?"

"Dad said I could stay in the off-season, but I only have a few more weeks until bookings start up again."

"Then what will you do?"

"Find an apartment, I guess. Somewhere with enough space to work from, too. You got any leads?" he cocks one eyebrow, and I know what he's hinting at, but I play along.

"I could ask around. What do you need for work?"

"A desk and a quiet spot. That's pretty much it," he says.

"What are you working on? Not exactly a lot of film studios around here."

"I've switched to audiobook production for now. Cameron knows a guy in that line of work who always needs new sound engineers so he can take on more contracts. I get the recordings, edit a few books a week, send them back. It's pretty easy actually, and the workload is more manageable. Plus, I can do it anywhere in the world."

He says that last part while sipping his wine, and refusing to look away. I could smack that smug grin right off his face.

"What?" he laughs. "What's that look about?"

"It's that easy? You quit your job and move across the world with a computer and a suitcase?"

"Yeah, turns out it is. Gave notice on my apartment, donated a bunch of stuff to Goodwill, booked the ticket, and here I am. I'm an idiot for not doing it sooner, frankly."

"What about when you get bored? Or Hollywood calls and offers you some once in a lifetime movie?"

"I'll tell them I'm unavailable. I'm with my girl."

His girl.

I can't even pretend to hate it. It's so sweet when he lets his mask drop, and it's only making me fall harder.

Ryan only has one drink with dinner, and after a dessert of *petit fours* from the local *patisserie*, he drives me up the road to my village and holds my hand while he walks me to my door. It's been a perfect evening, and despite my reluctance to be first to cave, I'm not ready for our night to be over.

I lean against the wall in the dim light of my communal hallway, and he plants one arm above my head. We stare at each other, both knowing we're about to cross some invisible point of no return. His eyes flutter closed, and he presses his forehead to mine, inhaling deeply.

"Ryan, please?" I sigh, pressing my hand over his heart.

"What is it, Bunny?"

"Kiss me?"

"I can't," he says, stepping back and leaning against the opposite wall. My jaw drops and he can't hide his satisfaction. He knows the effect he has on me. "I'm sorry, sweetheart. I'd really love to, but this is only our second date. We're still getting to know each other."

I scoff loudly. This is the man who had me half-naked on the kitchen counter less than fifteen minutes after bumping into each other last winter.

"I wouldn't want to rush anything and do something you regret, but I would love a third date if you have some space in your schedule."

"You're not serious."

"Oh, I absolutely am," he smirks, walking backwards away from me with his hands fixing the front of his trousers.

Inside, it takes under five minutes to bring myself to orgasm, and I come screaming his name like a curse.

Chapter 54
Kayla

THE MOUNTAIN IS BUZZING with people when the ski slopes open and she returns to her full winter glory. We've only had a few snow showers in the village, but there's still something so pure and childlike about stepping out of the house and catching snowflakes with my tongue.

Knowing things will be busy soon, I blocked today out in my calendar, wanting a day on the mountain that's just for me. The snowpack is still forming, but there's good coverage on some of the higher slopes, so I head out early to get my ski legs back before stopping at *The Marmot* for lunch.

The packed terrace is full of locals waiting for their first French onion soup of the season, and I stop to say hi to a few friendly faces. I'm about to head inside to order when I spot Ryan sitting on a deckchair, book in one hand, cold beer in the other.

My heart soars when I see him. That's my man, right there, chilling out and soaking up the winter sun like it's what he was born to do.

My man.

The thought is like a snowball straight in the face, a cold shower bringing me to my senses.

What am I playing at?

My body casts him in shadow as I approach, and he shields his hand to look up and see who stole his sunshine.

"Oh hi, Bunny. How are you?"

I've kept my distance these past couple of weeks, hiding when I see him in town, avoiding the chalet and Rico's in case I run into him there. But he's still here, and this is getting ridiculous.

I should be able to sit in his lap, kiss him freely, catch up on our days. More than that, I should have skied with him this morning, should have woken up in his arms and drank our morning coffee in our pyjamas with the radio on.

That's my man, and he's here in the mountains, and it's time to stop this nonsense.

"I'm ready for our third date," I tell him. He sets his beer down on the low plastic table next to him.

"Sounds great. Just name the time and place, and I'll be there."

"My house. Now."

His jaw drops, and he leans forward, but then crosses his arms and sinks back down again. "Ah, but I've got this beer, good book, and the view is super nice today. I don't know if you noticed."

I roll my eyes and kick his ski boot with mine. "Do you want to fuck me or not?"

He bursts out laughing, then has the nerve to pick his beer back up and finish it painfully slowly, his eyes locked on mine the entire time.

Once it's finished, he tucks his book inside his jacket pocket, wipes his mouth with the back of his hand, then reaches out for me to help him up out of the low deckchair.

We've spent many an afternoon laughing at folks struggling to get out of these while afflicted by a triple threat combination of ski boots, wet deck, and one beer at altitude.

I'm about to take his hand when I change my mind and start backing away. His brows knit together and he watches me hop down from the edge of the deck and run over to where I've left my kit in a sea of skis. Thankfully mine are custom, so they're easy to spot.

"Last one to the bottom's a rotten egg!" I yell back at him, fastening my helmet, then clipping my boots into my skis, grabbing my poles and shooting off down the hill. I always win our races, but there's never a prize, until now.

"You're a sneak, Kayla!" I hear him call after me, boots clomping on the wood as he runs to find his own skis from the stand. "You're gonna pay for that."

Here's hoping.

It's not the best head start, and the snow is still patchy in places where the morning crowd has swept up the perfectly groomed piste. If I wasn't so invested, I'd spin around and ski backwards, a skill I mastered at a much earlier age than him, and taunt him the entire way down.

There's not enough snow coverage in the lower part of the mountain, and it will be a few more weeks until we can ski right down to the chalets. My apartment is closer, but we still have to take a chairlift to get down the mountain, and I hurtle through the barriers with Ryan hot on my tail.

Thank God I found him early. In an hour or two, there'd be a twenty-minute queue for this lift, but most people aren't ready to give up on the mountain yet.

Once I'm in position, I wait for the four-seater bench to loop round and scoop me up. I'm certain I've won, until he barrels through the emergency stop barrier, ducking around the side and nudging me out of the way with the full force of his body.

The alarm sounds, the chairlift grinds to a halt, and Ryan gets an angry earful in French.

"*Désolé, désolé,*" he calls, holding up his hands in surrender. The lift operator resets the button, and kick-starts the mechanics, all those moving parts crawling back to life as we begin our descent.

"Think you can get rid of me that easily?" he says, clutching the side of my jacket and dragging me across the vinyl seating until I'm by his side.

We tuck our ski poles underneath our thighs, unclip our helmets and then his mouth is on mine, and my hands are in his gorgeous, messed up hair.

We make out like the teenagers we once were; all tongues and teeth and zero fucks given. We can't stop laughing, but we keep going, even when passengers on the way up whoop and cheer as we pass them, sending up a chorus of *'ooh la la'* and *'get a room'*.

I have a room, and once I get him in it, I'm never letting him leave.

Chapter 55

Kayla

Twenty Winters Ago / Age Eight

"That's not it," I tell him, turning him towards the chalet. "You're looking in the wrong direction."

"Am not. My grandma said you find the Big Dipper, draw a line with your finger and that's how you find it." He tips his head as far back as it will go.

"Well, *my* grandma said it's the brightest star in the sky."

"Then let's ask them and we'll see who's right."

We race down the hill to where they're drinking hot chocolate on the patio chairs behind Ryan's family's house. We always drink ours super fast so we have more time to build another snowman before they send us to bed. I'm getting really good at them now.

"Can you show us how to find the North Star again?" They make space for us to climb into their laps.

"Do you remember how to find the Big Dipper?" his grandma says, setting her mug down and pointing at the sky.

"See!" he yells. "I told you so." I poke my tongue out at him, and twist to follow the line of her finger.

"That's the North Star. And no matter where you are, if you look for it, you'll always be able to find your way home."

"*If* we're in the Northern hemisphere," Ryan says.

"Yes, Ryan," my grandma says, setting me down in her chair. "But let's hope you two friends are never half a world apart."

"Let me show you something very special our papas showed us when we were girls together." She crouches in front of us, lifting our warm mittens and pressing them against our chests.

Ryan and I look at each other, then back at her, trying not to laugh.

"No matter where your life takes you, if you're ever feeling lost or lonely, you can press your hand right here, and remember you sweet angels will always be two hearts, under one sky."

Chapter 56
Ryan

It's been six weeks since our third date, and in that time I've set up a home studio in Kayla's spare bedroom, moved all my stuff out of the chalet, and we've flown back to Edinburgh for Allie and Mel's wedding.

Spending more time with Kayla's friends was a blast, and I can't wait for them to come and visit us again.

Work has been just as busy as it was in L.A., but now when I clock off I get to curl up on the sofa with my girl instead of waiting hours to call her when she wakes up.

We've taken some time off for Christmas, and so far spent the holiday between our apartment and our parents' chalets. It's been so nice to catch up with them, Hannah, and Cameron, and I can't believe how much has changed since he and I flew out here last year. Absolutely nobody was surprised when Kayla and I told them we finally got our shit together.

Some nights her parents join us, others we all go to theirs, but with eight people around the table for dinner and card games, it feels like everyone is exactly where they're supposed to be.

This isn't our first Christmas together, but it is our first as a couple, and I'm keen to combine some of our old traditions with new ones. We've enjoyed French onion soup at *The Marmot* on more than one occasion, but we also decided to get new tattoos instead of gifts. Our thighs now sport matching North stars, high up on the inside. The design was my idea, the location was hers. A place only we would ever get to see.

Now it's time for our annual Christmas Day ski race, and we've paused at the top of our favourite mountain to take in the view and reflect on everything that's happened since last winter.

The skies are blue after a week of heavy snow, and I still need to pinch myself sometimes and remember this is my life now. Here, with her, I haven't missed my old life once. Well, maybe good Mexican food, but we make up for it with endless bread, cheese, and charcuterie.

"We haven't made a wishlist in a while," she says, leaning back against my chest.

I've been wondering when this might come up. Now we have all winter together, there's no rush to try new stuff in the bedroom, but it doesn't mean I've stopped thinking about things I want to do with her.

"I have a few things in mind," I tell her, and she tips her head against my shoulder, basking in the warm sun.

"Oh, yeah? Enlighten me."

I drop my mouth to her ear and speak slowly, so there's no mistaking my words. "I want a wife, and a dog, and some babies."

Kayla stiffens in my arms, and I take a step back, dropping to one knee as she spins around.

We've seen a few proposals on the mountain so far this winter, and she's always so happy to see people experience that special moment here. Though I'd love to do it somewhere a little more secluded, I think I've known for years my life was going to lead me to this place, to this moment, with her.

"Are you serious?" she gasps, bursting into tears when I produce a vintage ring box from the inside of my ski jacket.

"Kayla McInnes, there's no better view than you. No mountain I wouldn't move to make you happy. No world I wouldn't try to find you in if I even remotely understood the science behind many worlds theory. And clearly no cheesy metaphor I wouldn't try to wrangle into a proposal if it helped me convince you."

From the corner of my eye, I spot the photographer I've hired to take photos of this moment, as well as a few tourists who've whipped their phones out. I'm not normally a self-conscious guy, but until I have an answer, I don't think I can breathe.

"Will you marry me, Bunny?"

"Yes," she cries out, almost toppling me to the ground when she crashes into my arms. "I was going to say I think we should get a butt-plug."

Kayla is the one thing I know to be true, my solid ground, and still she finds ways to surprise me. She laughs through her happy tears, covering her mouth and looking around to make sure nobody heard her.

I slip the ring onto her finger, and she holds it up to watch it sparkle in the sun. The simple band topped with an emerald nestled between two diamonds has been cleaned and polished, but there was no time to figure out her ring size and get it resized. Thankfully, it fits perfectly.

"This is so beautiful, Ryan. I feel like I've seen it before somewhere."

"It was your grandmother's," I tell her, falling for her even more when her bottom lip wobbles. "She gave it to your dad before she died, apparently with an order that he could only ever give it to me."

"My dad gave this to you?"

"I know it's outdated, but I asked for his permission the night they got here, and he gave the ring box to me yesterday. I was planning to ask you at the New Year's fireworks display, but I couldn't wait a second longer."

"You're joking."

"I'm not, and I have something else for you, too."

Crouching down, I unzip my backpack, digging into the compartment at the back for the stack of papers tied with a bright red ribbon.

"What are these?" she asks, pulling at one loose end.

"That's every postcard you told me not to send." Months of them, double what I'd already mailed her.

"You still wrote them?"

"Sure did. Right up to..." I pull the bottom one out of the stack. "This one. I wrote it this morning while you were in the shower."

Watching her face light up when she reads it is the best Christmas gift of all.

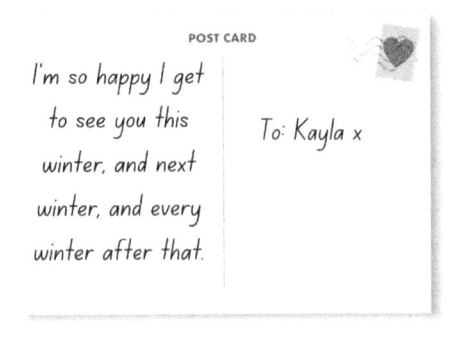

POST CARD

I'm so happy I get to see you this winter, and next winter, and every winter after that.

To: Kayla x

Chapter 57
Ryan & Kayla
Twenty-Eight Winters Ago / Age Seven Months

THE MOUNTAIN IS AGLOW with twinkling lights, but from the kitchen window of her alpine chalet, Juliette is only looking for two. All this curtain twitching, nosey business makes Celine laugh.

"They'll be here when they're here," she calls through from the living room, but Juliette waves her hand over her shoulder, dismissing her oldest friend.

In the distance, headlights wind their way up the hill, and Juliette holds her breath. Will they veer left towards the new ski-in, ski-out hotel on the outskirts of town? Or will they stay the course and head for the road that leads to her door?

She watches and waits, then bangs on the countertop, letting the curtain fall back into place. "It's them, they're coming!"

"Shhh!" Celine scolds. "There's no need for such noise."

Juliette throws the wooden door open wide, and races down the front steps without a care for icy patches or her safety.

When the car pulls into her driveway, a tall man with a bouffant head of dark hair steps out to greet her.

"Hi, Mum," he says, stretching his arms out to welcome her embrace. "It's good to see you."

"Yes, yes, good to see you too," she says, patting his chest and pushing him away. "Now give me the baby before my time on this earth is over. We were expecting you an hour ago."

His wife, Cheryl, appears from the other side of the car. "We got stuck behind a gritter for miles, I'm afraid."

Juliette yanks open the rear door, unclips the car seat, and lifts the sleepy boy into her arms. She nuzzles her face into his neck, inhales deeply, and looks to the sky with the happiest of tears in her eyes. Above her, nothing but stars.

She has met her grandson once before, when he was brand new in this world, all wrinkly and pink. Now, six months later, his cheeks are full, his hair is growing, and he sleeps without a troubled thought.

"Take him in before he catches a chill," Mark says. "I'll grab the bags."

Juliette is already half-way up the steps, filling the boy's head with promises of knitted bonnets and warm socks. In the entryway, she slips out of her boots and into the felted slippers that have trodden every inch of this house.

She hurries through to the living room, to where Celine waits on the sofa by the fire, her own granddaughter sleeping soundly in her arms. Juliette settles in beside her and they scoot closer together. It's the enviable intimacy of old friends who've shared a lifetime of memories, but never a moment like this one.

They adjust their holding positions until the two sleeping babes lay side by side on their laps. Juliette strokes the boy's fine tufts of hair, softly humming a French song her own grandmother sang to her.

The boy stirs, clenching and unclenching his tiny fists. The girl twists her head away then back again. They open their eyes, blinking, then smiling at the unfamiliar face in front of them.

"Kayla, this is my grandson, Ryan," Juliette whispers. "Ryan, this Kayla, the sweetest girl you could ever meet. You two are going to have the best adventures together. I know it."

THE END

Acknowledgements

While writing *See You Next Winter*, I counted that I've been in six long-distance relationships in my life. Some are best forgotten, one is still a friend, and one I'm happy to say was my very own endgame.

If you've been in a long-distance relationship, you'll know it's a unique experience to love, and be loved, but to have to show it from afar. Pulling on my own buried memories, my heart hurt for Kayla and Ryan while bringing them together, then tearing them apart.

LDRs are a brave thing to get into, worse if they're forced upon you by circumstance. I applaud anyone who's going through it.

My first thanks must go to readers of *Can I Tell You Something?* who charged into my DMs and demanded Ryan and Kayla's story. This book would not exist were it not for you.

A huge thanks to Gemma Flowers from The Lucky Type for more amazing work on this cover. To have such a beautiful duet on my bookshelf is a dream come true.

Thank you to my beta readers Brooke, Jill, Liz, Alex, Eloise, Nicola, Rachel, Katie, and Kristin for your early feedback, sense checking, and squealing.

A very special thank you to Brooke and Jill, who have supported me with author services and been my biggest cheerleaders over the last few months. You are the very best readers and secret keepers.

Thank you to my ARC team, my readers, my group chats, and my Instagram community. The way you carry me is unmatched, and I'm honoured to have your support.

And thank you to Alex, for everything, always.

Also by Holly June Smith

Snowbound Secrets
Can I Tell You Something? (Hannah & Cameron/Mac)
See You Next Winter (Ryan & Kayla)

Sunshine Book Club Series
The Best Book Boyfriend (Kara & Luke) – Read on for the first chapter
The Worst Guy Ever (Hattie & Rob)
The No Rules Roommate (Coming Spring 2025)

Standalone Romances
Just a Little Crush (Bec & Rennie)

The Best Book Boyfriend

Who needs real-life love when you have a shelf of perfect Book Boyfriends?

KARA HAS SWORN OFF men ever since The One dumped her without warning. Instead she spends her evenings reading books with guaranteed happy endings, crushing on fictional heroes who'll never let her down.

Luke is piecing his life back together after the death of his wife. Opening Sunshine Coffee was the first step, but he has no idea where to go from here.

When Kara stops by her new local coffee shop, Luke's clueless comments about the romance novel she's reading are the opposite of a Meet Cute. Determined to make a better impression, he asks for a recommendation to change his mind.

Three books later, he can see the appeal. Who knew reading about fictional people getting laid could teach you so much?

As their friendship blossoms into something more, their painful pasts threaten to keep them apart. But if romance stories have taught them anything, it's that there are many routes to love.

One road trip, a fake date, and a spicy readathon later, can Kara and Luke separate fact from fiction and find their very own Happy Ever After?

Chapter 1 – Kara

"Get in here."

My best friend Megan grabs our other best friend Hattie by her coat and yanks her inside my front door. "You'll never believe what's happened."

"Someone's dead?"

"Grim. No."

"Well, I know for sure nobody here is pregnant. Hashtag dry spell. Do you know, I think I've conquered every single man in a 30-mile radius? There are simply no men left."

Hattie sets down two paper bags full of food and takes off her bobble hat, pale pink hair spilling out over her shoulders. She undoes her buttons while Megan, a Golden Retriever in human form, bounces up and down on the spot beside her.

"Hmmm. Judging by your reaction, I'm guessing... did a new Taylor album drop?"

Megan wiggles from head to toe and can't contain herself any longer. "Even better. Kara got a guy's phone number!"

Hattie flings her coat to the floor, kicking off her boots in different directions as she scrambles through to the living room where I am curled up in the armchair in my favourite pyjamas. I cover my face with my hands, a strange mix of excitement and embarrassment churning away in my stomach.

Hattie drops to her knees in front of me. "What? When? Where? How? *Who*?"

"Get the food and I'll tell you." She rushes back to the hallway, and I head through to the kitchen to pull warm plates from the oven.

Every Friday night for the past year, these two sweet angels have come over to hang out with me. Hattie brings takeaway, Megan brings wine, I stock up on ice cream and popcorn. We eat, drink, pull out the sofabed, and make a nest to watch rom-coms in until we fall asleep. It started out as something Megan called my 'Healing Plan', but now it's just our routine, and the highlight of my week.

It all started the night my boyfriend, well, ex-boyfriend, left me. Adam left me after twelve (yes, 12!) years.

We'd been together since we were sixteen and we had it all. Fantastic chemistry, good sex life, great jobs, beautiful house. Except while I naively thought we were heading for marriage, babies, dogs, the whole shebang, he was hiring an assistant who, let's just say, helped him spread more than just his sheets.

I can still picture it like it was yesterday. He broke the news while I was plating up dinner from our local Nepalese restaurant, here in the kitchen of the house we bought and renovated seven years ago.

There I was, chatting away about our upcoming holiday like a total mug, and he just stood there holding a suitcase he'd already packed. He said he'd met someone else, and he was moving out. He didn't even say sorry. I heard he took her on the holiday instead. From his mum. Can you imagine how devastating that was? Not to mention humiliating.

The night Adam left, Hattie and Megan were here within the hour, and they both held me while I sobbed my heart out. I tried calling him over and over until Megan wrenched my phone from my sweaty, shaky hands. After crying so hard I'd thrown up in the kitchen sink, Hattie forced me to eat roti while I wailed that I'd never be able to have a takeaway again.

"He's not ruining takeaway for you, babe," she'd said. "No man can ruin takeaway."

After making it their personal mission to reclaim takeaway as a symbol of feminism and friendship, here we still are. Even though I'd never admit it to them, I do still get a bit of a lump in my throat if we're having Nepalese, memories of that night still just under the surface of my skin.

"So spill it!" Megan says, filling three glasses of Sauvignon Blanc nearly to the top. "She told me when I arrived, but has refused to give me more details."

"There's not much to tell," I say, but they are impatient, crowding around me. I must admit I am rather enjoying having a story to share that isn't just about work for once. "I was having coffee in that new place in the old haberdashers, and this guy came over and asked what I was reading. We spoke for a while, then he asked me for a recommendation and gave me a note with his number on it. That's it."

"Just some random guy?" Megan asks.

"He works there." I carry our plates, cutlery and napkins through to the low coffee table. Megan plumps floor cushions for us to sit on while we eat.

"He works there? What is he 21?" Hattie says, clapping her hands together, throwing up a prayer. "Oh God, please say he is 21."

"I think he might actually be the owner. Maybe mid-thirties."

"What does he look like?"

"Brown hair, bit of a beard, glasses," I bite my lip to stop myself from grinning. "Checked shirt, nice strong arms." I can't deny it. He was hot.

"Oh, she's checked out the arms," Hattie laughs. "You're done for."

"I'm gonna die," Megan mock faints onto my sofa. "And he just struck up a conversation about books? He's a real life Book Boyfriend!"

"No, no. Don't get ahead of yourself. He was a bit rude, actually."

"Ugh, men!" they both groan.

After he left, my calls to Adam went straight to voicemail. He blocked me on social media. Deleted me from his life. No wonder I've sworn off human men. Instead, I spend my evenings with an array of exceptionally hot literary ones.

"Every week a new Book Boyfriend." The girls tease me about my obsession with romance novels, but I've found a lot of comfort between the pages of these sweet and spicy tales of unlucky yet feisty heroines and the charming, attentive men who are feral for them.

If there's one thing the past year has taught me, it's that my bed, a good book, and a small but powerful collection of sex toys is all a girl really needs. And I get through a lot more than one book a week.

I take a big gulp of wine and Hattie spoons egg fried rice and crispy chilli chicken onto all of our plates. Megan opens the prawn crackers and takes dainty little bites, while I prefer more of a shovelling it all at once in approach. "So then what happened?" Hattie asks.

"Then I left."

"*Without the note*?" she gasps

"No, not without the note."

"Where is the note?" Megan asks. "We need to see the note."

"In my book in the front pocket of my bag," I whisper, tilting my head towards the door. The two of them lock eyes across the table, then leap from the floor, racing each other down the hallway. Megan lets Hattie take her down in a fit of laughter. Her big heart always wants everyone to win. Hattie reappears in the doorway moments later, note in hand, eyes frantically scanning what I know is his very nice handwriting.

"Oh, Jesus," she groans. "Why didn't you start with his name?"

"What's his name?" Megan turns to ask me but I can't answer her. I pull my jumper up over my face to hide my blushes. "Oh no. It's not Adam, is it?" Hattie just stands there, mouth on the floor, fully agog as she reads it again.

"Kara! What is his name?" Megan is up on her knees now, both begging and towering over me. I just curl myself into a ball waiting for Hattie to say it, but she gives the honour to me.

"It's Luke," I whisper.

"Shut the fuck up!" We are all wide-eyed and shriek as if possessed. Megan does not swear, *ever*, though I can understand her excitement.

Luke Russo is the hero in *To Love and Protect*, an Italian bodyguard with a scorching body and a filthy mouth. Though the girls don't read as much romance as me, they do enjoy an occasional recommendation, and my love for Luke Russo had me shoving copies into their hands. We've spent many hours talking about him, his muscles, the way he takes control, all the things we'd let him do to us. To meet a real life Luke, well, I know where their heads are going right now.

"I want him! Read it to me!" Megan says, and Hattie clears her throat.

"He's written his phone number and, and I quote, *'I look forward to having the time of my life. Luke.'*"

In seconds Megan is up and reading it over her shoulder, both looking back and forth between the note and me with faces full of joy. Hattie takes a deep breath as she sits back at the table and picks up her fork. "Kara, you're going to need to start from the beginning and tell us *everything*."

Printed in Great Britain
by Amazon